The Little Brownie House

and

Other Stories

by

ENID BLYTON

Illustrated by
Martine Blaney

AWARD PUBLICATIONS

For further information on Enid Blyton please visit
www.blyton.com

ISBN-10: 1-84135-467-8
ISBN-13: 978-1-84135-467-5

First published by Sampson Low (now part of Simon &
Schuster Young Books) as *Enid Blyton's Holiday Book Series*

This edition entitled *The Little Brownie House and Other
Stories* published by permission of Enid Blyton Limited

First published by Award Publications Limited 1993
This edition first published 2007

Published by Award Publications Limited,
The Old Riding School, The Welbeck Estate,
Worksop, Nottinghamshire S80 3LR

Printed in Singapore

CONTENTS

The Little
Brownie House

Kim and Mickle were very worried.
They were brownies who lived in a tree-
house – and now the woodman had
come to chop down their tree.

"We shall have to move," said Kim.
"And quickly too, or the tree will come
down and all our furniture with it!
Hurry, Mickle, and get it all out."

So the brownies took their furniture
on their shoulders and piled it on the
grass below. There it stood, and there
the brownies stood too, wondering
where to go.

They borrowed a handcart from
Bonny the pixie and put the furniture
on it, ready to wheel away. But there
really seemed nowhere at all to go.
There had been so many old trees cut

5

down in the wood that other people had taken all the empty houses there were.

"There's not even a hole in a bank we can have," said Kim. "At least, there's one – but the fox lives there, and he doesn't smell very nice."

"Oh, we can't go there," said Mickle. "We'd have to hold our noses all the time!"

"Well, let's wheel our barrow round a bit and see if there's any empty house we can go to," said Kim. So, with the noise of the woodman's axe ringing in their ears, they wheeled their cart away, with their two little beds, their two little chairs, their table, cupboard, curtains, and mats on it, looking rather forlorn.

They came at last to a high hedge. At the bottom was a gap, so they wheeled the barrow through – and there in a garden was a little empty house! It was painted brown, and had a big open doorway.

"I say! Look at this!" cried Kim, running to it. "An empty house – just

our size too! What about living here?
There's nothing in the house at all,
except some old straw."

"It's fine," said Mickle. "But it's
rather a funny house, Kim – there's no
door – and no window either!"

"Well, that doesn't matter, Mickle!"
said Kim. "We can easily make a door,
and just as easily make a window! Oh,
Mickle – it will be fun living in this
little house, won't it!"

7

Well, the two brownies moved in. The house was exactly right for them. They put in their beds, one on each side of the room, for the house had only the one room, "Our beds can do for couches in the daytime," said Kim.

They put the table in the middle, and the chairs beside it. They put the cupboard at the back, and spread the rugs on the floor. You can't think how lovely it all looked when it was done.

They had a tiny jam jar and Kim went to fetch some daisies for it. He put the vase of daisies in the middle of the table.

Mickle put the clock on the cupboard

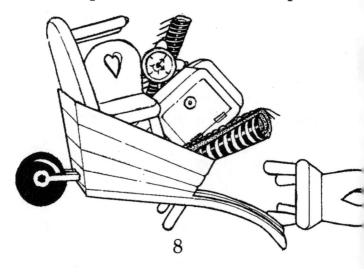

and wound it up. Tick-tick-tock-tock! it went.

"There now!" said Kim. "Flowers on the table – and a clock ticking. It's home, real home, isn't it!"

The brownies were very happy. The little house looked out on to a garden belonging to a big house built of brick. People lived there, and two children often came out of the house to play. But they never came to the brownies' house.

"It's a good thing our house is right at the bottom of the garden, where nobody ever comes," said Kim. "Now,

9

Mickle – what about making a door? The rain came in yesterday and wetted the mats."

So the two brownies set about making a door. They found a nice piece of wood, and with their tools they made it just the right size for a door. They painted it blue, and hung it on the doorway with two little brass hinges. It opened and shut beautifully.

They put a knocker on it and made a slit for a letterbox. It did look nice.

"And now we'd better make two little windows," said Mickle. "When we have the door shut our house is very dark and stuffy. We will make a little window each side and find some glass to put in."

So they carved out two squares for windows, and found some broken glass by the garden frames. They cut two pieces to the right size, and fitted them in. Then they cleaned the windows, and hung up blue curtains.

"Really, it looks simply lovely now!" said Kim. "The door is such a nice blue and the knocker shines so brightly, and the curtains at the windows look so pretty. I think we ought to have a party."

"Yes, we ought," said Mickle. "But if we give a party, we must make cakes. And we can't bake cakes unless we have an oven and a chimney – and there isn't a chimney, you know."

So they made a chimney, and bought

a nice little oven from the pixie down the way. They fixed it into the corner, and then lighted a fire. The smoke went straight up the chimney and away into the garden. It was marvellous! The oven cooked beautifully, and what a delicious smell came from it the first time that the brownies cooked buns and cakes!

They sent out the invitations to the party. "Everyone will love our little house," said Kim. "They will think we are very, very lucky to have found it. I do wonder who it belonged to. We have never heard."

Now, on the day of the party, Kim and Mickle began to do a great cleaning and cooking. All the mats were shaken, the windows were cleaned, the knocker was polished, and the stove cooked cakes, buns and biscuits without stopping. It was great fun.

And then something extraordinary happened! A voice outside the house cried out, "Look at this! There's somebody living here!"

The brownies peeped out of the window and saw two children, a boy and a girl staring in the greatest astonishment at their house. "Goodness!" said Mickle. "Do you suppose it's *their* house, and they want to come back and live in it? Oh dear, I do hope they won't turn us out!"

"We'd better go and ask them," said Kim. But before he could do that, somebody knocked at the door. They used the little knocker – rat-a-tat-tat! Kim opened the door. He saw the two children looking down at him in delight and surprise.

"Hallo!" said the boy. "Do you really live here?"

"Yes," said Kim. "I hope you don't mind. It was empty when we found it, and there was nobody to say who it belonged to. Do *you* want to come and live here?"

The children laughed and laughed. "No, you funny little thing!" said the girl. "Of course we don't. We live in that big house up the garden."

"Oh, then this isn't your house?" said Kim.

"It used to be our dog's kennel," said the boy with a giggle. "But we don't keep a dog now, so the kennel has been empty for a long time. Today we saw

smoke at the bottom of the garden, and we came down to see what it was. And we suddenly saw a chimney on our dog's kennel and two little windows, and a front door with a knocker!"

"We *did* get a surprise!" said the girl. "But oh, it's simply lovely! You have made the kennel into the dearest, prettiest little house I ever saw in my life!"

"So it was your dog's kennel!" said Mickle. "Oh, I do hope you won't want it for another dog."

"No, Mummy says dogs bark too much," said the boy. "So you're quite safe."

"May we really go on living here, then?" asked Kim.

"Of course," said the girl. "We'll never tell anyone about you, we promise. But please, please may we sometimes come down, knock at your door, and talk to you? You know, it's *awfully* exciting to have a brownie house at the bottom of our garden, with real brownies living there."

"You *are* nice," said Mickle. "Listen – we're having a party this afternoon. Would you like to come? You can't get inside the house comfortably, I'm afraid, but you could eat buns and biscuits out on the grass."

The two children squealed with joy. "Oh, *yes!*" said the girl. "Do, do let us come. We shall see all your friends then. And oh, little brownie, would you like me to lend you my best doll's tea-set for the party? It's very pretty, with a blue-and-yellow pattern."

"Thank you very much," said Mickle. "We haven't really got enough cups and plates, and we'd love to borrow yours."

So they borrowed the tea-set, and it looked fine in the little brownie house,

set out on the round table. The party was simply lovely – but the two who enjoyed it most were the children, as you can guess. It was such a treat to sit and look at all the little folk coming to the dog's kennel, dressed in their best, knocking at the blue door, and saying, "How do you do?" to Mickle and Kim!

I won't tell you the names of the children, in case you know them – because they don't want anyone else to visit the brownie house and frighten away their tiny friends. But don't you think they're lucky to have a dog kennel that is used by Mickle and Kim? Wouldn't I just love to visit there!

The Old
Red Cushion

Lisa's mother had been ill, but she was much better now. She was allowed to leave her room and go and sit downstairs in an armchair.

Lisa was pleased. It was lovely to see Mother down again, even if she did look rather pale and thin. The little girl fussed round her mother anxiously.

"Mother, which footstool do you want – or would you rather put your feet high up on a chair? Which pillow will you have? Or would you rather have a cushion?"

"I'll have that big cushion," said Mother. Lisa fetched it and tried to pack it gently behind her mother's back.

"It's rather a hard cushion," she said.

"You want a down cushion, Mother – they're so very, very soft. Like the one Granny has. It's a pity Granny lives so far away or I could go and fetch it for you. I'm sure she would lend it to you."

"Oh, this one will do all right," said Mother, but Lisa could see that it wasn't very comfortable.

"Perhaps Daddy could buy you a nice soft cushion, just for your back, Mother," she said. But her mother shook her head.

"No, dear – and don't ask him, whatever you do. He has had such a lot of expense with me ill for so long. He can't afford a luxury like a new down

cushion! I can easily make do with this one."

Lisa put a rug over her mother's knees and put her book beside her. Her mother thought what a kind, loving child she had. She smiled at her and Lisa smiled back.

"I do wish I could buy Mother a really soft cushion," thought Lisa, as she watched her mother trying to make herself comfortable with the big cushion behind her. "I know her back hurts her. I wonder how much money I've got in my money-box. I'll go and see."

She had two twenty pence pieces, a five pence piece and three pennies, but that was all. Forty-eight pence. Would that buy a cushion of any sort? Lisa felt certain that it wouldn't.

Still she went to the little village shop to find out. Mrs Bryan, the shop-keeper, shook her head. "No, my dear," she said, "I've no cushions at that price. You'll never get a down cushion for so little. They cost a great deal of money.

The cheapest cushion I've got is two pounds – and that's not a soft one either!"

Lisa went out of the shop sadly. It wasn't any good at all trying to get a nice, new, soft cushion. She went down the little winding street and came to the village sweet shop.

"I'll buy a few peppermint drops and take them to old Mrs Johns," she thought suddenly. "I always used to go and see her each week, but I haven't been once since I've been looking after Mother. She does so love peppermint drops. I'll spend twenty pence on them."

She bought the peppermint drops and set off to the tiny two-roomed cottage in which old Mrs Johns lived all by herself. She was a very poor old woman, but she managed to keep her cottage spick and span, and always had a vase of flowers on her table.

Lisa knocked at the door. "Come in!" cried Mrs Johns' rather quavery voice. Lisa pushed open the door and went in. There was old Mrs Johns, sitting knitting in her rocking-chair, rocking herself to and fro all the time.

"Well, if it isn't little Miss Lisa!" said the old lady. "That means your mother's a bit better, *I* know! Ah, I've wished I could send her something whilst she's been ill – but I haven't had a penny to spare, not one!"

Lisa knew how poor Mrs Johns was. Once, when she broke her teapot, she had to make her tea in a jug for three weeks, because she hadn't enough money to buy a new one. In the end Lisa gave her a little pot from her biggest doll's tea-set and Mrs Johns said it made the best tea she had ever had.

"I've brought you some peppermints," said Lisa and put them in the old lady's lap.

"That's kind of you," said Mrs Johns and opened the bag with trembling hands. "My, what nice ones! And how's your mother now? You tell me all about it."

Lisa told her. She told her about the cushion, too. "I've been trying to buy one for her, to put behind her poor back," she said. "But I've only got forty-eight pence – no, twenty-eight pence

now – so I can't. Daddy can't buy one either, because there are so many bills to pay since Mother's been ill."

"Ah, it's a hard world!" said Mrs Johns. "Do you know I've got to move out of here, Lisa? Yes, I have! My landlord's going to raise the rent, and I can't pay any more. So out I shall have to get!"

"Oh, Mrs Johns – but you love this little cottage so much!" said Lisa. "Wherever will you go?"

"I'll have to go to my niece, Sarah," said Mrs Johns gloomily. Lisa knew how she would hate that. Sarah was impatient and bad-tempered and would make life miserable for the old lady.

"Well, there now, don't let's think of such miseries!" said Mrs Johns, beginning to knit again. "Let's each

have a peppermint drop and talk of nicer things!" As they talked, Mrs Johns was thinking of what Lisa had said about the cushion. Her eyes went to the old sofa on which the little girl was sitting. There was an old red cushion there, very worn and shabby. But it was made of down!

"I've just thought of something!" said Mrs Johns, beaming. "See that old red cushion behind you, Lisa? Well, the inside of it is down! My old mother, she used to keep ducks, and she stuffed two pillows and a cushion with down. It's as soft as can be, that cushion. You take it for your mother."

25

"Oh – but I couldn't take your cushion!" said Lisa. "And I told you I've only got twenty-eight pence."

"Well, now, I'll tell you what to do with that money!" said Mrs Johns. "You spend it on some stuff to make a pretty, new cover! You can easily get some at the village shop. You can rip away that old red cover – it's shabby and faded and the edging is ragged. Then you can make a new cover and slip it on and sew it up!"

"Oh!" said Lisa, delighted. "Yes, I could. Oh, Mrs Johns – it's a lovely idea! But you shouldn't really give me your down cushion, I know you shouldn't."

"Oh, and who spent their money on buying me peppermint drops, I should like to know?" said Mrs Johns. "And who gave me the best teapot out of her doll's tea-set? And who ...?"

Lisa laughed. "Those were only little things," she said.

"And so is this only a little thing," said Mrs Johns. "You let me do a bit of kindness, too – it's not often I can, a poor old woman like me! Now you take that old red cushion home with you and on the way buy a nice bit of stuff to cover it with. Then you can rip off the old cover and put on the new one – and your mother will have a nice soft cushion for her poor back tomorrow!"

"*Thank* you," said Lisa, and took up the old cushion. "I must go now. I'll come and tell you whether I have made the cushion look nice or not in a day or two! And I do hope you won't have to turn out of your dear little cottage!"

"Ah well, I'm praying it won't be so," said the old woman. "It's nice to have your own little place when you're old."

On the way home Lisa bought some pretty red and blue stuff to make a new

cushion cover. She felt very pleased. Kind old Mrs Johns! Now Mother could have a really soft cushion.

At home that night Lisa set to work. She undid the old cover and slipped it off. Underneath was another cover, older still! It was a dirty green. Lisa took that off too.

"Oh dear – there's yet another one!" she said in dismay. "People have just put new covers on over the old ones – what a funny idea!"

As she was taking off the third old cover, something crackled underneath. Lisa felt it. It seemed like paper of some sort. How strange!

She took off the third cover – and
there, sewn into a kind of pocket on the
fourth cover, was a thin bundle of
papers! The little girl pulled them out.

They were five pound notes! Lisa
stared at them in the greatest surprise.
"Five pound notes! Heaps of them!
Whoever put them there?" she said in
surprise. "Gracious, I wonder if Mrs
Johns knows about these! I wonder if
it's too late to go and tell her."

Lisa was so excited that she slipped
out of the house straight away and ran
down to the village. Mrs Johns was
most surprised to see her.

"Mrs Johns! Look what I've found
inside your old red cushion!" cried Lisa.

"First there was the red cover, then there was a green one and then a third one – and sewn in a kind of pocket on the fourth cover were these five pound notes!"

"Five pound notes – heaps of them!" said old Mrs Johns. "So that's what happened to my old mother's savings! She always did say she'd hidden them away safely – but nobody knew where. And when she died, very suddenly, we could never find them."

"So they belong to *you*! Oh, Mrs Johns, now you won't have to leave your little cottage, will you?" cried Lisa. "You will have plenty of money to pay more rent."

"So I shall, so I shall," said the old woman, and a tear ran down her cheek. "To think of such a thing! Oh, Lisa, it was the kind thought you had for your

mother that's brought all this good luck!"

"No, no – it was *your* kindness in giving me your down cushion!" cried Lisa. "Oh, I'm so glad for you, Mrs Johns."

"Now you take five of these," said Mrs Johns. "You buy a fine present for your mother – and one for yourself!"

"Oh no!" said Lisa. "That's a lot of money!"

"I feel rich now," said Mrs Johns. "I can repay my friends for the kindness

they've so often shown me. And it's a wonderful feeling to return a bit of kindness, Lisa. You take the money now, straight away, and give me a bit of pleasure tonight, thinking of the fine presents you'll buy!"

But Lisa would only take one five pound note, to spend on her mother. She would spend it on fruit and a book. She sped home to tell her mother all about it.

She finished covering the cushion. It was so soft – exactly what her mother wanted behind her back!

"It's really lovely, dear," said Mother, leaning back on it. "Just right. Thank you so much for covering it for me so beautifully! And now I must write a little note to thank Mrs Johns for her kindness to me! I really can't let her give you a five pound note to spend on me, poor old lady!"

But Lisa did spend it on her mother, and how she enjoyed it! She bought her grapes one day and a peach the next, and a new book the next. How nice it

was to feel really extravagant like that!

Mrs Johns didn't have to move, of course. She had plenty of money now to pay more rent. Lisa went to see her the next week, and there, sitting on the sofa, was the biggest doll she had ever seen!

"Oh, what a beauty!" she said. "Is it for one of your great-nieces, Mrs Johns?"

33

"It's for a little girl I know," said Mrs Johns. "I've called the doll Lisa after the little girl! It can shut and open its eyes, and all its clothes come off, right down to its vest. And look at its real eyelashes and its tiny fingernails! You'll be her mother, Lisa, so see you look after her well!"

What do you think of that? Lisa could hardly believe it. She picked up the doll and nursed her. "I don't deserve you," she said "I really don't!"

But Mrs Johns said she did – and I agree with her, don't you?

The Mouse
and Rat Robber

Mr Tickle, the brownie, had a very large house. He had a lot of servants to keep it clean and tidy for him. There was Mrs Trim the cook, Lucy-Loo the housemaid, Tippy the kitchen-maid, and Miss Needle the little sewing-maid.

Now one day Mrs Trim the cook went down the garden to get some parsley. It was a nice, warm day in the early spring and the birds were beginning to sing. Mrs Trim sang a little song, too, as she went.

She passed the woodshed – and suddenly she stopped. She heard a noise in there! What could it be?

Scrape, scrape, scrape, scrabble, scrabble, scrabble, went the noise. Then it stopped. Then it started all over again. Scrape, scrape, scrape ...

"Oooh! A mouse!" cried Mrs Trim and gave a squeal. She couldn't bear mice. She knew they wouldn't hurt her. She knew a mouse would be far more frightened of her than she was of the mouse, but just because once, when she was a child, she had seen a grown-up scared of a little mouse, she was, too. So she stood there and squealed. "Oooh! A mouse! I hope it won't come out under the door."

Lucy-Loo came running down the garden when she heard Mrs Trim

squeal. "What's the matter?" she cried. "Have you hurt yourself?"

"There's a mouse in the woodshed!" said Mrs Trim, and she pointed at the shut door with a trembling finger. "I'm sure there is. Oh, what shall we do, Lucy-Loo?"

Lucy-Loo gave a squeal, too. "A mouse! Oh, quick, let's go before it runs at us!"

Scrape, scrape, scrape, scrabble, scrabble,scrabble!

"It must be a very big mouse to make all that noise," said Mrs Trim, beginning to tremble. "Do you think we ought to tell Mr Tickle?"

Tippy the kitchen-maid came down the garden to see what all the fuss was about. The others told her.

"There's a mouse in there! Just fancy that! We're so scared, Tippy."

Tippy screamed. She didn't know why she screamed, but she saw that the others were frightened, so she thought it would be a good thing to scream. Her scream made them jump.

The noise in the woodshed stopped. "You've frightened it, Tippy," said Mrs Trim. "Oh, I hope it won't come running out."

The noise suddenly began again and everyone jumped. Scrape, scrabble, scrape, scrabble.

"That's too big a noise for a mouse to make," said Tippy. "Much too big. It must be a rat, not a mouse."

Well, that made everyone squeal even more loudly! A rat! Terrible! "Rats bite, don't they?" said Mrs Trim, and she went quite pale. "Oh dear – are we going to have the place running with rats and mice? We shall have to tell Mr Tickle."

Miss Needle came running down the garden to ask what the matter was.

"It's a mouse!" said Mrs Trim.

"No, a rat!" said Tippy, quite enjoying herself now. "Oh, it's awful, isn't it! A rat in the woodshed! I'll never dare come and get firewood now."

SCRAPE, SCRABBLE, SCRAPE, CRASH!

All the four women jumped. What a noise! And what was that crash at the end? Something had overturned. They stood and listened, trembling. They heard a hissing noise. Then there came

39

the sound of wooden boxes falling –
thud, crash, thud.

"It's not a mouse or a rat, it's a
burglar!" cried Lucy-Loo.

"There's a man in there!" squealed
Tippy.

"I'm going to faint," said Mrs Trim.

"We must fetch Mr Tickle," said Miss
Needle.

They rushed off down the garden,
Tippy giving little squeals all the way.
They found Mr Tickle, the brownie,
standing looking very cross indeed in
his study.

"Where have you all been?" he said sternly. "The dinner is burnt up on the stove. I've been ringing the bell for at least ten minutes."

"Oh, Mr Tickle – we thought there was a mouse in the woodshed!" began Mrs Trim.

"Don't be foolish," said Mr Tickle. "It won't hurt you."

"But then we thought it must be a rat!" said Lucy-Loo, giving a little scream at the end. "Oh, Mr Tickle, a rat! Oooooh!"

"Silly girl," said Mr Tickle, looking crosser than ever. "It was shut in the woodshed, wasn't it? Why didn't you get the dog and open the door of the shed?"

"Well, we don't think it's a rat now," said Miss Needle. "Mr Tickle – we think there's a robber there! There was *such* a noise! Oooh – a robber! How can we sleep in our beds at night?"

"Fiddlesticks, rubbish, stuff and nonsense!" said Mr Tickle, getting more and more angry. "What do you mean by

41

all this silly fuss? Here's the dinner burnt, and all of you in a state of trouble! You want shaking. You want –"

"Oh, don't scold us, Mr Tickle," wept Mrs Trim. "Oh, look – there's the village policemen – both of them together. I'll call them in and they can arrest the robber." Before anyone could stop her, Mrs Trim had run out into the road and called in the policemen. They looked rather astonished, but when they heard there was a robber to arrest they were quite pleased. "By the noise in the shed there might be *two* robbers," said Tippy, and she gave another squeal.

"One more squeal from you, Tippy, and you catch the next bus home and stay there," said Mr Tickle.

Tippy didn't squeal again. They all went down the garden, Mr Tickle leading the way. They came to the woodshed.

"Who's going to open the door?" said Mrs Trim. "Oh my – there's the noise again!"

Sure enough, there was a noise in the woodshed – a scrapy noise, and then a hiss. Mr Tickle listened and then he laughed.

"Ha ha, ho ho, he he! I will now show you the mouse-rat-robber!"

He turned the handle and flung open the door. The two policemen got ready to catch a robber if one appeared.

Then, in the darkness of the shed, everyone saw something crawling round, something that carried a big shell on its back!

"It's my tortoise," said Mr Tickle. "I put him in a box up on the shelf to sleep for the winter – and I suppose he woke up on this mild day and thought he would like a walk. So he gave one of his little hisses and tried to scrabble his way out of the box. When he did get out, he knocked a lot of things down – see them on the floor! And he fell down himself and began to crawl all over the place."

"Oh," said Mrs Trim and felt ashamed of herself.

"It's a pity none of you opened the door and looked to see what was making the noise," said one of the policemen, quite disgusted.

"Wasting our time like this!" said the other.

The tortoise crawled out into the sunshine. "So you've woken up at last!" said Mr Tickle. "Well, take a walk if you like. Eat some grass for your dinner – you'll be lucky to get any dinner. Mine is all burnt up."

Mrs Trim went red. So did Lucy-Loo. Tippy hid behind Miss Needle.

"We will none of us have any dinner," said Mr Tickle, "unless, of course, you like to eat it now it's burnt. Any more fuss about a mouse-rat-robber that doesn't exist, and you'll all pack and go home. I hope you are ashamed of yourselves! To think that not one of you had the pluck to open that door – why, the six-year-old girl next door would have come in to do it for you." Mr Tickle walked off.

"I shan't be silly about mice or rats again," said Mrs Trim. "Here we've lost a good dinner, got two policemen in for nothing, and nearly lost our jobs. All because we were afraid of a mouse that wasn't there!"

What would *you* have done? Opened the door and peeped in? Of course you would, and so would I!

The
Talking Doll

Uncle George brought the wonderful doll home with him from somewhere far away. "Guess what I've got for you!" he said to Sarah. "Just guess!"

As soon as he put the long box on the table Sarah guessed. "A doll! Oh, Uncle George, is it a big doll?"

"Right first time," said Uncle George. "It's the most beautiful doll you've ever seen, Sarah. And she looks so real you would almost think she was alive. She stands, and she walks just like you do!"

He took off the lid – and there, lying down in the tissue paper, was the most wonderful doll Sarah had ever seen in her life. She was a big doll, with dark brown curly hair, blue eyes with real eyelashes that curled down and then

up, just like Sarah's, and a pretty smiling mouth that showed white teeth.

"Uncle! It's the loveliest doll I ever saw!" cried Sarah and she gave Uncle George a hug. "Oh, isn't she beautiful! I shall keep her all to myself and never, never let anyone even hold her!"

"Oh, you mustn't be a selfish little girl," said Uncle George at once. "You must share her with your friends. They will all love her too. You share her, Sarah!"

48

"I couldn't!" said Sarah, taking out the lovely doll and cuddling her. "She's mine, all mine. I shall call her Princess Marigold because she looks like a princess doll."

Princess Marigold was certainly the finest doll that anyone in that town had ever seen. She was not only beautiful, but she was clever. She stood steadily on her two feet just like you – and if you turned a key three or four times in her back she began to walk across the room, putting one foot in front of the other in such a life-like way that everyone cried out in surprise to see her.

She could open and shut her eyes, too, and she could look at you in such a real manner that sometimes people thought she must be alive. Sarah was delighted with her and very proud indeed.

She gave Princess Marigold her best dolls' cot, and she washed all the sheets and blankets so that the new doll could have a nice clean bed. She dressed and undressed her, and brushed her pretty hair twice a day. Nobody could have looked after a doll better than Sarah did.

At first Princess Marigold was very pleased to be living with Sarah. "What a good, kind little girl!" she thought, as she cuddled down into the cot that night and shut her lovely blue eyes. "I am lucky to live here."

But after a while she changed her mind. Sarah was good and kind to her doll because she was so proud of her and wanted to show her off to all her friends . . but she wasn't very good or kind to anyone else. She was rude to her mother, she was disobedient, she was rough with the girls and boys who came to tea with her. In fact, she was one of those unpleasant children that all of us have met at some time or another.

Princess Marigold was shocked at her behaviour when Allan, Pam and Karen came to tea to see the new doll. As soon as her mother had gone out of the room

Sarah began to show off and be silly.

She pulled Allan's tie undone. She undid the back of Pam's dress and wouldn't do it up again. She pulled off Karen's hair slide and hid it. All the time she giggled and chattered, showing off in such a stupid manner

that Allan began to think about going home. "I shall go home if you act like that, Sarah," he said. "Don't be so silly."

"Yes, she's silly," chimed in a voice. "She's often silly! She's the silliest girl I ever saw. You go home, Allan."

Sarah spun round in a rage and looked at the three children. "Who said that? Who said I'm silly?"

"I don't know," said Allan, puzzled. "I didn't."

"Nor did I," said Pam, and Karen shook her head, too. Nobody knew that it was the doll, Princess Marigold, who had spoken.

"I shall tell my mother about you!" cried Sarah, stamping her feet.

"Tell-tale!" called the voice again. "Sneak. Tell-tale!"

"You're not to call me names!" shouted Sarah, and she went to the toy-cupboard door, sat down beside the toys there, and began to pull them out. "I shan't speak to you! I shan't play with you! I shan't show you my new doll."

"Baby! Spoilt baby!" said the voice, and Pam, Allan and Karen looked at one another, puzzled. Which of them was saying all this?

They heard the sound of little footsteps and turned. It was Princess Marigold, walking over to them. The three children gave a cry of delight.

"Oh, what a lovely doll! Oh, how clever she is! Look at her walking!"

Sarah swung round in a rage. "Who set her walking? Don't you dare to touch my new doll!"

But by this time Princess Marigold was right over by the children and they were all kneeling down, petting her. She blinked her eyes at them as if she was quite real.

"She seems almost alive!" said Karen. "Oh, come on to my knee, Princess Marigold!"

But before she could take the doll on her knee Sarah pulled her roughly away – and the doll fell to the ground.

"She's always rough!" complained the doll. "What she wants is a good slap!"

"How dare you say things like that to me, Pam – or was it you, Karen?" cried Sarah. "I'll smack you!"

And she gave both the startled girls a slap each. Karen began to howl – and in came Sarah's mother at once. "What's

the matter? What are you doing?"

"She took my doll," wailed Sarah, who always got her complaint in first. "She's a bad girl, Karen is!"

"No. *You're* the bad girl!" said the doll. "You're telling stories, too. You're very, very bad!"

Sarah's mother didn't know it was the doll talking. She thought it was one of the children. "Oh, Sarah," she said, "surely you haven't been rough with the others? You know that they are your guests!"

"You're not to take their part, Mother, you're not to!" cried Sarah, and she lost her temper. "You're horrid, too. I don't like you!"

"Isn't she really disgusting?" said the doll in a loud voice. "I never saw such behaviour in my life. Why doesn't somebody punish her?"

Sarah's mother looked very uncomfortable. She thought that Allan, Pam or Karen was saying all this. Oh dear – had Sarah got into one of her rough moods again? "Now, now," she said, "we won't say horrid things, any of us. We'll go down to tea. The doll can come, too."

So Princess Marigold went with the children, though she did hope she wouldn't have to sit next to Sarah. She rather liked Allan. She thought he was a nice boy.

Marigold was put between Sarah and Allan. Tea began. It was a nice tea, and there were chocolate buns, which were Sarah's favourites.

Sarah was greedy. She helped herself to all she wanted, but she didn't bother about looking to see if the plates of her guests were empty or if she could pass them anything.

"Look after your guests, dear," her mother said.

"Oh, Mother, don't fuss so," said Sarah rudely. "They can look after themselves!"

"Fancy talking to her mother like that," said Marigold in a loud voice that made everyone jump. Nobody guessed it could possibly be the doll. They all wondered which of them had spoken.

"And isn't she greedy?" said the doll. "And such bad manners, too! Never offers anyone anything. I expect she will gobble up more chocolate buns than anyone!"

Sarah burst into tears. "Mother! Why do you let people talk like that about me! I won't have Allan, Pam or Karen to tea with me again. I won't!"

She got down from her chair, dragging the tablecloth with her as she did so and upsetting the cups of milk. "There she goes again!" said the doll. "Rude and careless and clumsy! Spoilt child!"

"Who said that?" cried Sarah in a rage. The children shook their heads.

"I didn't," said Allan. And Pam and Karen said the same. Then Allan said something surprising.

"I believe it's your new doll," he said. "I'm sure it is! After all, if she is clever enough to open and shut her eyes, and stand up, and walk, she may be clever enough to talk too. I'm sure it's Princess Marigold."

"Oh no, dear, it can't be!" said Sarah's mother, smiling. "Dolls could never say things like that. Sit down again and behave yourself, Sarah."

"I shan't," said Sarah, and she snatched up the doll and ran out of the room. "And it *isn't* my doll talking! It was Allan, I'm sure! He just said that so that he wouldn't be blamed for saying horrid things about me! I won't play with any of you."

She ran upstairs and sat down in a chair, tears of anger in her eyes. She put the doll on the floor beside her.

"Well, you ought to be ashamed of your behaviour!" said the doll in a severe voice, and looked up at Sarah out of her big, blue eyes.

There was nobody in the room except Sarah and the doll. Nobody at all. So Sarah knew for certain that it *must* be the doll talking! She glared down at her.

"So it *is* you who can talk like that! That's a marvellous thing for a doll to be able to do – but just hold your tongue unless you have nice things to say to me!"

"I shall go on saying exactly what I think," said Marigold. "It's time somebody did. You're a spoilt, selfish child, and nobody tells you so. So I shall go on telling you so till you stop behaving so badly!"

Sarah looked down at the doll. What a very, very peculiar thing! Fancy having a doll who could really talk! Sarah felt cross with Marigold for saying such things to her – but she couldn't help feeling pleased to have such a very clever doll! How she would boast about her at school! But she must certainly stop her from being so horrid to her.

"You can talk all you like," she said to Marigold, "but I warn you – if you say one single horrid thing about me I'll put you straight to bed!"

"I don't stay with children like you," said the doll scornfully. "I can walk. I shall walk away."

"You're a very, very bad doll,"

said Sarah angrily. "I've a good mind to undress you, put your nightdress on, and put you into your cot!"

"Don't you dare!" said Marigold, and she stamped her little foot. Then Sarah snatched up the doll and began to undress her.

"All right!" she said. "You just see what I do with bad, naughty dolls!"

The doll struggled hard. Sarah tore her pretty dress as she took it off. She took off the petticoats and vest, and pulled her nightdress over Marigold's head. Then she set her roughly on the floor.

"I'll get your hairbrush," she said. "And first I'll brush your hair and then I'll hit you with it."

But Marigold was not going to stay a moment longer. She got up, and began to run towards the door. And there she met Allan, Pam and Karen just coming in!

"Stop her, stop her!" shouted Sarah.

"No, let me through!" cried Marigold. "I won't live with such a horrid girl. I'll find somebody else! Let me through!"

The children stood aside, and she ran down the passage and came to the stairs. She slipped and fell. She rolled down the stairs from top to bottom, then picked herself up and ran out of the garden door.

"I know where the gate is!" she panted. "If only I can get there before Sarah."

She did, because Allan tried to stop Sarah, and by the time the angry little girl got downstairs the doll was nowhere to be seen.

"Where did she go? Has anyone seen

her? Stop her, stop her!" cried Sarah.
But nobody had seen Marigold slipping
out of the gate, and Sarah had to go
crying back to the nursery.

"She's run away," she sobbed. "In her nightdress too. And oh, she was so beautiful and so clever! I can't *think* why she should run away from me!"

Well, Allan, Pam and Karen could think of the reason quite easily, but they were too polite to say it. They thought they had better say goodbye and go home. And on the way home they laughed.

"Fancy a *doll* telling Sarah what she thought of her!" said Allan. "And running away, too. I only wish she'd come to *my* home!"

She didn't go to Allan's home, or Pam's or Karen's. I suppose she was afraid of meeting Sarah again if she did. But she must have gone to somebody's, and I'd *love* to know whose!

The
Sparrow Children

Once in the very cold weather, the young sparrows could not get enough to eat. They were not yet a year old, and they were not as clever as the older sparrows at finding seeds, and bits, and scraps.

"We will go to our fathers and mothers, who fed us in the nest last year, and see if they will help us," said Beaky, the biggest young sparrow.

So they flew off to where the older sparrows sat on the barn roof, waiting for the farm hens to be fed. Then there was a chance of flying down and stealing a few grains of corn.

"There are our fathers and mothers," said Tailer, a tiny sparrow. "Mother! Don't you remember me?"

The big brown sparrow he spoke to looked at him in surprise. "Oh, you are the naughty little sparrow that would keep trying to fly from the nest before you were allowed to!" she said. "Yes – I do believe you are! What do you want?"

"Please, Mother, we young sparrows are getting more and more hungry in this frosty weather," said Tailer. "We want you to give us food as you used to do when we were first out of the nest."

"Good gracious! We can't do that now that you are nearly a year old!" said the older sparrow. "You must look after yourselves!"

The young sparrows were sad and disappointed. Now what were they to do?

A small brownie, who was running by, stopped when he saw the unhappy sparrows.

"What's the matter?" he said. They told him, and he nodded his head.

"Many people are hungry now," he said, "as well as birds. But I am very lucky. I have plenty of food stored away

– enough to share with you if you like."

"Oh, you *are* kind!" cried the sparrows. "May we come now?"

"Yes," said the brownie. "You may come once a day, at dinnertime. I will cook enough potatoes in their skins for all of us, and I will bake enough bread for us all too. Come along!"

They flew on to his small shoulders, and on to his red-capped head, chirruping gaily. He took them to a

small house set right underneath a bramble bush, so well hidden that nobody could see it if they passed by.

"Now," said the brownie, getting some hot potatoes out of the oven, "here we are! Potatoes for everyone!"

He looked round his room. There was only one chair. He pointed to his bookcase and the sofa. "The boy sparrows can sit on the bookcase and the girls on the sofa-back," he said. "But, dear me – you all look exactly alike to me! However am I going to tell one from another?"

"I'm a boy sparrow," said Tailer, sitting on the bookcase. "And Beaky's a boy sparrow too. But Toppy, Flick, Feathers and Fluff are girl sparrows. All the rest are boys."

The brownie stared at them. "I shall never know which is which," he said, "and I do want to know you all properly. *I* know! I will give the boy sparrows little black bibs to wear! That will always show me which are the boys."

He took eight little black bibs from a drawer, and put them on the boy sparrows. They were delighted. They really did feel grand. The girls wanted them too, but the brownie shook his head. "No," he said, "if you *all* wear black bibs I'll be just as much muddled as before."

He gave each sparrow some potato and a handful of crumbs. They were so hungry that they gobbled them up at once.

"Can we keep our black bibs on?" begged the boy sparrows, when they had finished. "We do feel so grand in them."

"If you like," said the brownie, smiling. They did look so funny with the bibs on. So they all flew off, and the boy sparrows showed their new bibs very proudly to everyone.

Each day they flew to the brownie's, and each day he fed them until the warm weather came.

"Now you can feed yourselves," he said. "But come again next year, as many of you as you like, and I'll help you; but in return, please bring me as much thistledown as you can in the autumn, because I need plenty for my eiderdowns and cushions!"

So in the autumn the sparrows hunted for thistledown for the brownie, and in the cold New Year weather he fed them with all kinds of food.

And they wore their bibs – and still do! You don't believe it? Well, please look carefully at all the sparrows you see. Those that have black bibs under their chins are the boy sparrows – and those that have no bibs are the girls. The boy sparrows always begin to wear them in the New Year, so you will see plenty of them. And now you will always know cock and hen sparrows when you see them!

71

Billy's
Butterfly

It was February, and the winter was going fast. All the children were glad, because it was much nicer to come to school with the sun warm on their heads than with snow or sleet whirling round.

Miss Jones was giving a nature lesson. At the end she said, "Now, I do really want you to use your eyes and ears this spring term. There is such a lot to see out of doors. Please look about this week, and on Friday bring me whatever interesting things you have found."

"We shan't find any flowers, surely, Miss Jones?" said Billy.

"Oh yes, you will, if you look," said Miss Jones. "You'll find groundsel, anyhow, and maybe a blossom or two of golden gorse out on the common. And if you listen you will hear the chaffinch beginning to sing his spring song and the tits calling loudly."

Billy wasn't very good at nature. He hadn't learnt to use his eyes and ears well. Birds might be singing madly all round Billy, but he didn't hear them. He might walk over half a dozen different flowers, but he wouldn't see them.

But Billy liked Miss Jones very much, and he really did long to please her. He wanted to get good marks in nature. That would please his mother, too. So he made up his mind that he really would go for walks after afternoon school and look about for something interesting.

But that afternoon his mother wanted him to stay indoors because his aunt was coming after tea. Then, next afternoon, he had such a lot of homework to do that he knew he wouldn't finish it until bedtime. So there would be no time for a walk.

"Never mind," said Billy to himself. "Tomorrow is only Thursday. I'll go tomorrow. It's fine and sunny today, so

some flowers may be out tomorrow."

But, alas, when tomorrow came his mother had a job for him to do. "Billy," she said, "the bicycle shed is so full of odds and ends that I can't get my bicycle out quickly when I want to go shopping. Will you tidy it up for me after tea, dear?"

"Oh, Mother, I did want to go for a walk really," said Billy. "But, never mind, I'll do the shed quickly, and then perhaps there will be time."

"Thank you, dear," said his mother. So when Billy had had his tea that day he ran out to the little bicycle shed. It was a dark little place, with only one

small, rather dirty window. And what a mess it was in!

"Oh dear, no wonder poor Mother can't get her bicycle out quickly," thought Billy, as he began to tidy the shed, piling up pots and boxes, and folding up sacks in a pile. "My goodness, this job will take me ages!"

It did take him ages! It was dark before he had finished, and then it was no good going for a walk, because he wouldn't be able to see anything at all! Billy was disappointed. Now he wouldn't be able to take anything to Miss Jones, and she would be cross, and he wouldn't get any marks.

"Still, it's no good being cross about it," thought Billy, as he picked up a broom to sweep the cobwebs away from a corner of the shed. His mother had given him a candle in a candlestick to light up the shed whilst he finished it. He swept down a cobweb, and then, to his surprise, something fluttered down from the corner and came to rest on his hand.

"What is it?" said Billy, half-scared. He held up his hand to the light of the candle – and, to his enormous surprise, he saw that a beautiful butterfly was resting on his hand, its brilliant wings opening and shutting very gently. Billy stared in astonishment.

"A butterfly! At this time of year! However did that happen? It must have been in that cobwebby corner. Gracious, what a surprise!"

The butterfly stayed on Billy's hand. The little boy began to feel excited. "My goodness me – what will Miss Jones say when she sees this? It's better than any flower, and better than any bird-song! Anyone can find flowers and hear birds

77

– but who else will find a butterfly at this time of year?"

Billy called his mother loudly. "Mother! Mother! Come here quickly and bring a small cardboard box!" His mother hurried out in surprise, carrying a little box. Billy showed her the butterfly.

"Oh, how lovely!" said his mother. "Are you going to take it to show Miss Jones, Billy? Keep quite still while I get it into the box."

Soon the butterfly was in the box, and there it slept safely all night. In the morning Billy took it proudly to school. He didn't say a word about his find to

anyone until Miss Jones took the nature class.

Harriet had heard the chaffinch calling, "Pink, pink", and George had seen two sparrows with black bibs under their chins.

"Good boy," said Miss Jones. "The little cock sparrows always grow bibs of black feathers under their chins in the New Year."

Jane had brought groundsel with many little yellow brush-like flowers. Rosie had brought chickweed with dozens of tiny white starry flowers.

"I've got some early snowdrops," said Robert proudly. "Out of my own garden, Miss Jones!"

"Lovely!" said Miss Jones. She gave the children marks for their finds. At last it was Billy's turn.

"And what have you to show us or tell us, Billy?" asked Miss Jones.

"I've got this to show you!" said Billy, and he took out his cardboard box from his desk. He opened it – and out flew the gorgeous butterfly, fluttering round the room. All the children shouted in surprise and delight.

"Oh, oh! A butterfly! In wintertime! Oh, Billy, how lucky you are! Where did you get it?"

"Well," said Billy, "I meant to go for a walk each afternoon this week and see if I couldn't find some flowers. But Thursday came and I hadn't. I was going to go for a walk after tea on Thursday when Mother asked me to tidy up our bicycle shed. Well, I couldn't say no, could I? So I did what she asked me to – and when I was sweeping a cobweb down from the wall this butterfly fluttered on to my hand!"

"It's a peacock butterfly," said Miss Jones. "A real beauty. Billy, some butterflies, like the peacocks and the red admirals, sleep all the winter through – and this butterfly of yours must have chosen your shed to sleep in.

They like dark corners for their winter sleep."

"I was lucky, wasn't I?" said Billy.

"Well, you were kind to your mother and did a job she asked you to do," said Miss Jones, "and good luck came to you through your own kindness. I shall give you top marks, Billy – top marks for doing a good job, and top marks for finding a butterfly. Well done!"

Billy *was* pleased. I wonder if you've got any sleeping butterflies in the dark corners of *your* shed, too?

I Was
Here First

"Take my white ducks to the pond on the green," said Mr Flip to Bong, his servant.

"Take my goat to graze up on the common," said Mrs Flap to Bing, her servant.

So Bing set out from his end of the village of Woosh with the goat, and Bong set out from his end of the village with a row of white waddling ducks.

Now to get to the pond and to the common each had to climb over a stile. They met at the stile at exactly the same moment.

Bong threw out his chest and put his leg on the step to climb over before Bing.

Bing at once put his nose in the air

and stepped on the stile to get over before Bong.

"I was here first," said Bong, glaring.

"Indeed you were not!" said Bing.

"You always were one to push yourself first, no matter where you are!" said Bong.

"And there isn't a person in Woosh who hasn't had your elbows poked into him in a crowd!" said Bing.

"You're a very rude person," said Bong. "I've a good mind to report you to Mr Plod, the policeman."

"Well, go and report me now, and I'll

84

be able to get over the stile!" answered back Bing smartly.

"You think yourself very clever, don't you?" said Bong angrily. "Let me pass!"

"I'm going to climb over first!" said Bing, and he actually put his leg over the stile. Bong put his, too. Then they had to sit on the top of the stile, because neither could get over whilst the other was there. They glared at one another again.

"I shall box your ears," said Bong at last.

"Try it," said Bing fiercely. "I'll give you such a punch that you'll fall off and screech for help."

They sat there, sulking hard. Neither of them quite dared to hit the other. "If I sit here all day I shan't let you climb over before I do!" said Bong. "So put that in your pipe and smoke it."

"I don't smoke," said Bing, "and if I did I wouldn't bother to put anything in my pipe that *you* said! It's well-known that you are the stupidest fellow in the village."

"Ho! Well, whose grandmother can't read?" yelled Bong.

"Yours!" said Bing at once. "And whose father once tried to build a house and put the roof on first? Ho, ho, that was a joke!"

"What dreadful untruths you make up," said Bong. "You're not worth talking to."

"And you're not worth listening to!" said Bing. Then, because they couldn't think of anything to say for a minute they both sat in silence, their noses in the air. They had forgotten all about their ducks and goat. The ducks wandered off through a gap in the hedge and found the village pond. They got in and began to swim happily.

The goat made its way through the gap, too, and found a nice patch of grass up on the common. It was soon eating contentedly.

Presently along came old Mr Stamp-About. He was a bad-tempered old fellow, as everyone knew. He was surprised to see the two servants sitting

on the stile, side by side. "Hey, you!" he said. "What are you doing, wasting your time like that? Come on down and let me get over."

Neither Bing nor Bong moved. Each was afraid that if he did the other would hop over at once. So they sat and stared at Mr Stamp-About.

He stamped in anger. "Are you deaf and dumb? Get down off the stile and let me over!"

"Er – you get down first, Bing," said Bong.

"No. You get down," said Bing.

"After you!" said Bong, pretending to be polite.

"What's all this!" cried Mr Stamp-About and he stamped again. "Get down off that stile at once! Sitting there like that, preventing people from passing. I never heard of such a thing!"

"Well – you see," began Bong, "it's like this. I got here first, and ——"

"What do I care which of you got here first!" cried Mr Stamp-About and his face turned red with rage. "Take that, Bong – and you take that, Bing! *Now* will you let me pass!"

He shook Bong so hard that Bong fell off the stile. Then he pushed Bing's face and Bing fell off the stile, too. They both hit their heads hard on the ground

and yelled loudly. Mr Stamp-About climbed over the stile, treading heavily on both Bing and Bong, and disappeared over the field.

"I'm hurt!" wept Bong. "Look at this awful bruise."

"And I'm sure I've broken my leg," said Bing and tried to stand up. He limped a few steps. Then he suddenly stopped and looked all round.

"Where's the goat?" he said, looking scared.

"And where are the ducks?" said Bong, his eyes nearly popping out of his head.

"They're gone!" said Bing. "What will Mrs Flap say when I get back and tell her I've lost the goat?"

"And what will Mr Flip *do* when I tell him I've lost his ducks?" groaned Bong. "Oh my – why were we so silly?"

They both went groaning back to Mr Flip and Mrs Flap. "What, my ducks lost!" cried Mr Flip. "Well, you go and look all over the countryside and find them, Bong – and not a bite do you get till you bring them home!"

"My goat gone! Well, you go and hunt everywhere for it!" cried Mrs Flap to Bing. "Not a meal do you get till you bring it home behind you!"

Bing and Bong set off, sore and hungry. They hunted here and they hunted there. They walked for miles looking for the ducks and calling for the goat. And at last, in the evening, Bong found the ducks swimming gaily on the village pond not a minute's walk from the stile. And Bing found the goat on the common not a minute's walk from the stile, too!

Bong collected the ducks. Bing called the goat. They began to make their way home – and they met at the stile again.

"After you, Bing!" said Bong, in a most polite voice.

"No, no – I've learnt my lesson this time!" said Bing. "After you, please!"

"My dear Bing, I wouldn't dream of climbing over first," said Bong.

"And you may be sure I wouldn't push over in front of *you,*" said Bing.

An angry roar disturbed them. It was Mr Stamp-About coming home from his day's visit to his sister. "WHAT! You still here! You just wait and I'll knock your wooden heads together till they drop off! You just wait!"

But they didn't wait! They both climbed over at exactly the same moment, lost their balance, fell to the ground, howled, and picked themselves up. Then they rushed off in different directions, the ducks waddling in surprise after Bong, and the goat capering round Bing. What a pair!

"Ninnies!" burst out Mr Stamp-About. "Woodenheads! Donkeys! Geese! That's what they are!"

And really, I think he was right, don't you?

91

In The
Fashion

The Wizard Ho-Ho
  Used always to fly
On a magical carpet
  Up in the sky.

But now that's old-fashioned
  And Wizard Ho-Ho
Says magical carpets
  Are really too slow.

And so he has ordered
  His servant to bring
A little blue saucer –
  What a strange thing.

But see, the old Wizard,
   So clever is he,
Is making the saucer
   As LARGE as can be!

How right in the fashion
   Is cunning Ho-Ho.
Swift through the heavens
   His saucer will go!

She Hadn't
Any Friends

There was once a girl called Linda who hadn't any friends. She was an only child, so, as she had no brothers or sisters, and no friends either, you can guess she was lonely.

Nobody asked her out to tea. Nobody asked her to play on Saturday mornings in their garden. Nobody wanted to walk home with her from school.

This was rather strange because there was nothing really the matter with Linda. She wasn't rough or rude or spiteful or boastful – she wasn't any of the things that make children dislike somebody. She spoke nicely and she had good manners, and she was quite a pretty child too.

"It's strange," said her mother. "Linda is quite a nice little girl – and yet nobody likes her. Nobody makes friends with her. So, poor child, she is terribly shy and hardly knows how to play at all!"

But the person who worried about it most of all was poor Linda herself! When she saw Mary and Jane running off together, she felt ready to cry. They never shared a joke with *her*. And when

95

George asked Anne to tea, and told her he was going to have his clockwork railway out especially for her, Linda simply longed and longed to see it too. But George didn't ask her once.

One day Kevin came to school with a lovely new pencil that had a screw top. If you screwed it one way the pencil wrote red. If you screwed it the other way it wrote blue. Kevin showed it to everyone. But he didn't show it to Linda. Linda was longing to see it. She kept at the back, hoping that Kevin would say, "Linda, look!" But he didn't.

"Now why didn't Kevin show me his pencil?" wondered Linda sadly. "There

must be something dreadfully wrong
with me, because I've no friends at all.
Not a single one! I'll have to do
something about it."

Now, you know, the world is made up
of two different kinds of people. One
kind just sit down and mope and do
nothing when difficulties come – and
the other kind think about them hard,
and find some way of beating them.
And luckily for Linda, she belonged to
the second kind of people.

So she sat down and thought about it. "I don't know, myself, why I've no friends – and Mother doesn't know, or she would help me," thought Linda. "If I could find somebody who did know, they might be able to tell me what to do. I can't go on and on never having any friends – it's too lonely and miserable."

Now Linda's teacher at school was Miss Brown, who was very nice indeed. She was strict, very fair, and always kind and patient. Linda liked her, though she was just a bit afraid of her.

"Miss Brown knows a tremendous lot about everything," said Linda to herself. "She really does. I'll go and tell her my worries. She might be able to tell me what to do."

So after tea that evening Linda ran along the road to Miss Brown's house. She knocked at the door. Miss Brown opened it. She was surprised to see Linda.

"Come along in," she said. "What's the matter? Anything wrong?"

"There is, rather," said Linda. "I don't know quite how to tell you – but oh, Miss Brown, it does worry me so dreadfully that I haven't any friends at all. I think and think about it. Is there anything horrid about me?"

Miss Brown laughed. She took Linda into her sitting-room. She was sorting out all kinds of tangled silks for the sewing-class the next day. She went on with her work, and listened to Linda.

"But *is* there anything horrid about

99

me?" asked Linda. "Please, please do tell me if there is."

"There is nothing horrid about you," said Miss Brown. "Nothing at all. But there isn't anything very nice either! You're an in-between person, Linda – not nice, and not nasty either. Just a little in-between."

"Oh," said Linda puzzled. "I don't quite know what you mean! How can I be nice if nobody is nice to me?"

"Now listen carefully, Linda," said Miss Brown in her kind voice, as she sorted out the silks. "There is only one way in this world to make friends – yes, only ONE way – the way to make friends, Linda, is to BE one. Be a good friend to everybody, and they will be good friends to you. You are never

unkind enough to push anyone over –
but on the other hand, you are never
kind enough to rush to help somebody
up when they have fallen. You leave
someone else to do that."

"I see," said Linda. "It isn't enough
to sit back and wait for other people to
be friendly. I've got to go right out and
be friendly myself."

"That's right," said Miss Brown.
"Now look – here am I, sitting sorting
out tangled silks. If Mary or Jane had
been here they would have said. '*I*'ll
help you, Miss Brown,' and I should
have felt so warm and friendly towards

101

them. But you, silly little girl, sit there with your hands in your lap and say nothing about helping me – so you don't make me full of warm, kindly feelings towards you. That's not my fault – it's yours."

"Oh, Miss Brown!" said poor Linda, going red with shame. "I *did* think of helping you – but I thought you'd say no."

"Well, you might have given me a chance to say no or yes," said Miss Brown. "Don't be a little in-between any more – neither nasty nor nice. Even if people say no to you, never mind. You will at least have *tried* to be nice. Now, think of Sophie – she's a naughty, untidy, careless little girl, not nearly so good-mannered or neat as you are, and yet all the children love her. She rushes to everyone's help. She's interested in everybody. She takes books and toys to children who are ill. She just *will* be a friend, so everyone is a friend to her. Now what about you trying to do the same thing?"

102

"Will people be friends with me if I do?" asked Linda, who was now busy sorting out the silks, and quite enjoying it.

"I can't promise you that," said Miss Brown. "But at least they will take some notice of you. We haven't any idea what you are really like, you see. You just sit at the back of the class and say 'Yes, Miss Brown,' and 'No, Miss Brown,' and I don't believe that some of the children think you are real! Be a real person for a week, and see what happens. Don't mind being laughed at, and don't mind being pushed aside. Just make up your mind to be friends with everyone, no matter what they say or do."

"I will," said Linda, and she went home feeling excited and pleased. Now at last she was going to find out if she could get any friends. It seemed so simple when she thought about it.

"The only way to make friends is to BE one," she said again and again to herself. "Why didn't I think of that before?"

Linda felt quite excited when she got up the next morning. She rushed off to school early. On the way she met Billy and John. Billy was telling John about his new kitten. Neither of the boys took any notice of Linda.

"Do you know, my kitten climbed up on to the bookcase where Mummy keeps her bowl of goldfish – and it put its paw in to catch the fish!" said Billy. Linda walked beside Billy, listening.

"Tell me some more of the naughty things it does," she said.

Billy stared at her in surprise. "Do you like kittens, then?" he asked.

"I love them," said Linda. "Tell me all the things your kitten does."

104

Well, Billy was quite ready to do that. All the way to school he told about the bad things his kitten did, and Linda listened.

"You ought to come and see my kitten," said Billy, as they went in at the school gates. "I haven't got a name for it yet. You could think of one perhaps. Come after tea and see it, will you?"

Linda's heart jumped for joy. That was the very first time anyone had ever said, "Come and see it."

"I'd love to," she said.

As they all took their things off in the cloakroom, untidy little Sophie came in, panting because she was late. She flung her satchel down on the form – and it burst open. Out flew all her pencils, rulers, pen, books, and everything. "Oh dear, I'll be later than ever!" she said, and knelt down to pick them up.

Linda flew to help. "I'll pick them up while you hang up your things," she said. "Then you won't be late."

"Oh, thanks awfully, Linda," said

106

Sophie. "You *are* a sweetie!"

Linda went red. It was a funny thing to be called a sweetie, but she liked it. She picked all the things up and put them back into the satchel. Then she went off to the big hall. Sophie came after her and slipped her arm in hers. "I should have been late if it hadn't been for you!" she said.

Nobody had ever slipped their arm through Linda's before. It was a lovely feeling.

There was painting that morning. Somebody always had to put out the water in the little pots. Linda put up her hand when the painting lesson came.

"May I fill the water pots for you, Miss Brown?" she said, feeling quite nervous at hearing her own voice.

"Thank you, Linda. That would be kind of you," said Miss Brown at once.

Linda got the water in a little jug, and filled each pot without spilling a drop. It was really nice to be doing a job for the class. She had never offered to do one before.

"I'm getting on," she thought. "It's not so hard as I thought it would be." But the next thing that happened wasn't quite so easy.

It was playtime, in the middle of the morning. The children were going to play policemen and robbers. Kevin was the head of the policemen, and he called out the names of the children he wanted. Mary was the head of the robbers.

"I'll be a policeman, Kevin," said Linda eagerly. Kevin looked at her.

"I don't want you," he said. "You wouldn't be any good."

Linda went red and felt very small. She went to Mary.

"Can I be on *your* side?" she asked.

"No, thanks," said Mary. "You're no good at games."

Well, that was rather dreadful. "But I suppose it's my own fault for never joining in before," thought Linda. She stood watching the others play. It looked so exciting. One of the robbers came squealing by her. It was Jane. As

she went by, she caught her foot on something and fell over. Down she went with a crash!

Linda ran up to her, hoping that Jane wouldn't push her away. "Oh, you've hurt your knee," she said. "Come with me and I'll bathe it for you."

Jane was crying. She was glad to lean on Linda's arm. She limped into the cloakroom and Linda bathed the knee for her. "Have you got a hanky?" she asked Jane.

"No, I've lost it," said Jane.

"Well, I'll lend you mine," said Linda. "It's one of my best ones, but never mind!" She bound up Jane's knee very well indeed.

"I never knew you were so kind before, Linda," said Jane, surprised. "Thank you. I'll bring back your hanky quite clean. I can't play policemen and robbers any more. Let's go and play a quiet game together in the garden."

So the two of them played together. Jane took Linda's arm when the bell went. "If my mother says you can, will you come to tea with me tomorrow?" she asked. Linda beamed joyfully.

"Oh, *yes*!" she said. "Thank you."

Linda felt happy for the rest of the morning. After school the children went to their cloakrooms to get their coats and hats. Linda wondered if any of the children would ask her to walk home

111

with them. She didn't quite like to ask anybody herself, for they all had their own special friends. But nobody asked her. It was disappointing.

"Still, I can't expect to have everything all at once," thought Linda. She was just going to leave, when she saw John rushing back.

"Linda! Have you seen my scarf? Mother said she'd be very cross if I didn't bring it home – and I nearly forgot it."

"No, I haven't seen it," said Linda, and was just going to walk off when she noticed how worried John looked. She stopped. "I'll help you to look for it if you like," she said.

"Oh, I say, thanks!" said John, and the two of them began to hunt around.

Linda found the scarf at last, hung up on somebody else's peg. John was so pleased.

"You've saved me from getting into a row," he said, as he wound it round his neck. "I didn't know you were so nice, Linda. Walk with me on the nature ramble this afternoon, will you?"

Linda sped home, delighted. She was going to see Billy's kitten after tea. She was going to walk with John in the afternoon. And she might be going to tea with Jane the next day. Her mother was most surprised to see such a happy face. Linda usually looked so very solemn and serious.

"Mother! Can I help you to lay the dinner?" cried Linda, ready to do anything for anybody, she felt so happy.

"Oh, darling, how sweet of you to

113

want to help me," said her mother in surprise. "Yes – get the plates and the glasses, will you?"

As Linda ate her dinner she thought happily of the other children. Why, they were as nice and friendly as could be, after all! Miss Brown was quite right. She looked at her mother, a splendid idea coming into her head.

"Mother! Do you think I could give a little party soon?" she asked. "I've got some money left over from my birthday – I could buy a balloon for each child, and perhaps a box of crackers, if you can't afford to."

Linda's mother was astonished. Why, Linda always said she had no friends to have at a party before – and now here she was, asking for one!

"Of course you can have a party," she said. "It would be lovely if you could buy balloons and crackers. I will buy the cakes and the sweets and make lemonade for you."

"I'll ask the children this afternoon," said Linda. So she did. Everyone was

114

surprised, but oh, how pleased! Boys and girls do so love parties, and Linda had never given one before.

"I'd love to come," said Hilary. "Thank you awfully."

"And I'd love to come too," said Robert. "And you must come to mine. It's on the twenty-third. Don't forget."

"And when I have *my* birthday party, I'll ask you too," said Sophie, slipping her arm through Linda's. "Linda, you seem quite a different person this week. You're just as nice as anyone else!"

Linda asked Miss Brown to come too. Miss Brown looked at the little girl and smiled.

"Yes, I'll come," she said. "I shall like to see you giving balloons to all your friends. How does it feel to have plenty of friends after having none at all?"

"It's wonderful," said Linda, slipping her hand into Miss Brown's. "It wasn't very difficult either, Miss Brown. I'm glad you told me what to do!"

And today is Linda's first party. She has spent all her money on brightly-coloured balloons, two boxes of crackers, and a little present for everyone, even Miss Brown. You should just see her in her blue party dress looking pretty and happy, standing at the door to welcome her friends.

"Yes, my *friends!*" she thought. "I've plenty now. Oh, how I wish I could tell everybody that the quickest way to make friends is to BE one. I'd so like everyone to know."

Well, I'm telling everybody for her. It's a very good idea, isn't it?

The
Whispering Pool

Once upon a time there was a boy called George who badly wanted to wish a wish that would come true. He knew what he wanted to wish – he meant to wish that he could have a hundred wishes! Then he really could have a very good time, get presents for everyone, and wish everything he wanted for himself.

But somehow he could never find out how to make a wish come true. He tried all sorts of things, and wished hundreds of wishes – but they never came true.

And then one day he met Bron the Brownie. He was walking down a path in Cuckoo Wood, one that he had never been down before, and he suddenly saw Bron coming towards

him. He stopped in surprise, for he
knew quite well that the little man was
a real, live brownie, the kind he had
often seen in books.

"I say," said George, "I say – are you
a brownie? You are, aren't you?"

"Of course," said Bron, stopping.
"What do you want? Anything I can do
to help you?"

"Oh, *yes*," said George. "I want to
wish a wish that will come true. Can
you give me a wish like that?"

"No," said Bron. "But I'll tell you
where you can get one. You must go to
the Whispering Pool in the very heart
of the wood, and if you can hear what it
says, and do what you are told, you can
get a wish."

"How can I?" said George, feeling
very excited.

"Well, if you do what the Whispering
Pool tells you, and dip your hand in to
drink from it at the end, you will find
that whatever wish you wish will come
true at once," said Bron. "I've often got
wishes there. Look – see that path? Go

straight down it, turn left by the three oak trees, turn right by the path of primroses, and go on to the end. You'll find the Whispering Pool then all right."

Off went George, feeling so excited that his knees shook. He turned left at the three oak trees, and right by the primroses, and then went straight on.

And then he came to the Whispering Pool! It was a strange place, a little brown pool set in a shallow hole in a rock. It shook and shivered and wrinkled and bubbled all the time.

"It's magic, there's no doubt about that!" said George, looking deep into it. He saw his own face looking back at him, made crooked by the ripples. He listened hard.

And he heard a bubbling whisper coming up from the strange little pool.

"Stir me as many times as there are hours in day and night! S-s-s-s-s-stir me!"

How many times did George stir the pool? He took a stick and carefully stirred the brown waters round and round, twenty-four times.

The pool bubbled tremendously, and the bubbles burst with funny little pops at the surface. A green mist came from them.

"It's awfully magic!" thought George. "I wonder what I do next?"

A low sound came from the pool again, half a gurgle, half a whisper. "Blow on me, and spell the word 'Thunder' three times!"

"Gracious!" thought George. "How do you spell thunder? Yes, I think I know." So he blew on the surface of the Whispering Pool, and spelt the word "Thunder" three times.

"T-H-U-N-D-E-R!"

And when he had spelt it out three times the Whispering Pool blew up into a kind of little storm, and a low, thundery sound came from it. It was very peculiar. Then its surface calmed down, and it became so smooth that once more George could see his face there.

"What next?" said George to the pool. "Tell me, quick!"

"Go to the oak tree and bring back the fruit it bears!" whispered the pool suddenly. "Put it into me and stir till it is dissolved!"

"The fruit of the oak tree – what's that?" thought George. He ran to an oak tree and looked up at it. The tree was bare, for it was wintertime, but on it grew little round knobs of brown.

"Oak-apples!" thought George. "That must be the fruit!" He picked one, and was just running back to the pool with it when he stopped. He remembered a nature lesson he had had that autumn about the fruits of different trees.

"The oak-apple *isn't* the real fruit of the oak tree!" said George out loud. "It's the acorn that is the fruit! Goodness, I'd have spoilt the spell if I'd dropped in this oak-apple."

He ran back to the tree and looked under it on the ground. He found an acorn, still in its cup. He was very pleased. He picked it up and ran back to the pool with it.

He dropped it in, and then stirred the little brown pool till the acorn seemed to have disappeared. "I didn't know before that acorns could melt like sugar," thought George, astonished. "This pool must be very, very magic."

It was. It suddenly turned a bright green and sparkled brightly. A voice came out of it again, whispering like the trees in summer.

"Now dance round me seven times seven! Then drink deep!"

George felt so excited that he could hardly dance round the rock in which the strange pool lay. "Seven times seven. Now what are they?" he thought, beginning to dance solemnly round the pool. "Oh, dear, I wish I'd learnt my tables better. I'm supposed to know right up to twelve times, but I'm not at all sure of seven times. Seven sevens are ... seven sevens are ... oh, yes of course, they are fifty-two."

So George carefully danced round the pool fifty-two times, counting out loud as he went. "One ... two ... three ...."

At the number seven the pool changed to blue. At fourteen it changed to yellow. At twenty-one it changed to red, and at twenty-eight it changed to purple. When George chanted thirty-five it shone golden, and at forty-two it shimmered like a diamond. At forty-nine it turned to brilliant silver, and shot silvery bubbles high into the air.

But when George stopped at fifty-two it had changed to its first brown colour and lay quite still. "Now," thought George, "now to drink it! Then I'll have to wish a wish – and I'll wish for a hundred wishes – and what a time I'll have! Won't I surprise everyone!"

He dipped his curved hand into the pool, lifted the brown water to his mouth and drank. It had no taste at all. "There!" said George. "I've drunk from the magic pool. Now I'll wish. Well – I wish that I may have a hundred wishes, and that all of them may come true!"

He stood for a moment – then he wished the first of his hundred wishes.

"I wish I was back at home!"

But nothing happened at all. George was in the wood by the pool, he wasn't back at home. He wished the same wish again, and still nothing happened. It was most disappointing.

Then he wished another wish. "I wish a little brown pony would appear so that I might ride him home!"

But no pony appeared, though George waited patiently for ten minutes. "Something's gone wrong," said George, very sadly. Then he wished a whole lot of different wishes, but not one of them came true.

George walked home miserably. On the way he met Bron the Brownie again. "Hallo!" said Bron. "Did you get your wish all right?"

"No," said George, and he told him all about it, what he had done, and how careful he had been. Bron laughed.

"You were all right till the last thing you had to do," he said. "Seven times seven are fifty-two indeed! Why don't you learn your tables? Eight years old,

aren't you – and you don't know your
seven times! For shame! Now you've
missed a lovely wish, for you'll never
find that wishing pool again."

"I shall look for it again and again,"
said George. "I'll find it one day – and
by that time I'll know how to spell any
word I'm asked, and I'll know all my
tables, yes, even my thirteen times!"

But George has never found that
Whispering Pool again. They say that
people can only find it once – so if ever
you chance to come across it, be sure
you know your seven times table. *Do*
you know what seven times seven are?

It's Just
a Dream

Tippy and Heyho had been sent shopping by their Aunt Minnie. They had a long list, and they were cross about it.

"Our basket will be awfully heavy," said Tippy gloomily. "Bother Aunt Minnie – always sending us out on errands!"

Heyho looked at the list. "Potatoes – they're always heavy. Plums – they're heavy too – and I bet we'll have wasps round us all the way home! A sponge cake – well, that would be all right if we could carry it inside us instead of in our basket!"

Tippy grinned. Then he nudged Heyho. "Look out – there's Mr Plod, the policeman. We'd better go another way. He's been cross with us ever since we crossed the road when the lights were red and made all the cars hoot at us."

"I don't like Mr Plod," grumbled Heyho. "Always scowling at us. Always complaining to Aunt Minnie whatever we do. I wish I could throw something at him."

"Sh!" said Tippy. "He might hear you. I don't like Mrs Surly either. I'm sure she'd hit us if she could. Just because we threw our empty ice-cream cartons into her garden!"

129

"Well, I suppose we should have put them into the litter-bin," said Heyho, "only it was such a long way to it. Horrid old woman. I'd like to throw something at her too."

This was a very naughty way to talk, of course. They went on chattering like this till they got to the shops. They bought the potatoes and the plums, and got a very nice cake indeed, with icing on the top and three cherries in the middle of the icing.

"Now the basket is frightfully heavy," said Heyho with a groan. "Are you carrying your fair share, Tippy? My arm is almost pulled out of its socket."

They left the little village and went on down a country lane. And then they had their first surprise.

Just round the first corner they met a big brown bear! Tippy and Heyho almost dropped the basket in surprise. They trembled as the bear came towards them. It waved its paw, did a funny little clumsy dance, and went past them down the lane.

"Did you see what I saw, Heyho?"
said Tippy in a frightened voice.

"I saw a bear," said Heyho. "And he
waved his paw at us!"

"I don't like it," said Tippy. "Come
on, let's go on quickly, before it comes
back. What are people thinking of to let
bears wander about like dogs!"

131

They went on – and round the next corner they had their second surprise. They met a baby elephant, waving its trunk, ambling along in a very carefree sort of manner.

"Oooh!" said Tippy, clutching Heyho. "Now there's an elephant! Can you see one too, Heyho – a baby one?"

"Yes," said Heyho, watching the creature go past him down the lane. "What's happening, Tippy? Are we dreaming?"

"I think we must be," said Tippy. "You always meet things like bears and elephants and lions and tigers round corners in dreams."

"Well, I hope we don't meet a tiger or a lion," said Heyho nervously. "I don't like this. And how is it we are dreaming the same dream? It's odd."

"We're not really," said Tippy. "I expect *I'm* dreaming the dream, and you happen to be in it, that's all. You must be part of my dream."

"I'm *not*," said Heyho indignantly. "I'm having this dream, too. I *saw* the bear and the elephant just as much as you did!"

"Look – there's a kangaroo jumping over the hedge in the next field!" said

133

Tippy, startled. "Fancy me dreaming a kangaroo too!"

"Yes – it really *is* a kangaroo," said Heyho in amazement. "I do hope we really *are* dreaming, Tippy."

"Don't be so silly – of course we are," said Tippy. "Did we ever meet wild creatures like this before when we went shopping for Aunt Minnie? It's just a very real and peculiar dream. I shall wake up in a minute and turn over in bed and tell you all about it. See if I don't."

"Oh, Tippy – there's a lion!" said Heyho, clutching at Tippy's arm. "Quick, let's hide!"

"No," said Tippy boldly. "It's only a dream lion. I'm going to shout 'BOO' at it – and it'll run away!"

So he shouted "BOO" at the lion – and, dear me, it looked extremely startled and turned tail and ran away! "There you are – what did I say?" said Tippy. "It's a dream, all this! Come on, Heyho, let's enjoy ourselves. Let's be naughty! We shall soon wake up, and it won't matter a bit."

"Well – let's eat this lovely cake first then," said Heyho. "It will probably taste just as nice in this dream as it does when we're awake."

So they ate the cake. It was delicious! The icing melted in their mouths.

"Well – for a dream-cake that was absolutely delicious," said Tippy. "I'm sorry we didn't buy two. I say, Heyho – we needn't bother to take these potatoes and plums home to Aunt Minnie, as it's only a dream we're having. Let's do something naughty with them!"

"Oooh, yes," said Heyho. "Let's throw some plums at Mrs Surly's chimney-pot! I bet I'll hit it before you do!"

So the two of them went back to Mrs Surly's cottage. They began to throw plums up at the rather crooked little chimney-pot. But, of course, neither of them hit it. The plums went right over the low roof of the cottage and fell into the garden behind.

Mrs Surly was there, hanging out her washing. She was very surprised indeed

when ripe plums began to fall all round her – and very angry when one hit her on the head and burst.

"What's all this?" she shouted, and ran to see who was throwing the plums. She couldn't believe her eyes when she saw it was Heyho and Tippy. She picked up her stick and ran at them, shouting.

They giggled. "All the same, we'd better run," said Heyho. "A stick might hurt, even in a dream. Goodbye, Mrs Surly!"

They rushed off back to the village, laughing. Mrs Surly simply couldn't understand their behaviour. She put on her hat and set off to complain to their Aunt Minnie about them. Aha! Aunt Minnie would deal with them all right!

The mischievous pair caught sight of Mr Plod, the policeman, walking slowly down the street. "Quick – see if we can knock off his helmet with potatoes!" cried Tippy. "It's only a dream; we shall wake up before he catches us! We might as well have some fun."

So they aimed two large potatoes at Mr Plod – and Tippy's potato hit his helmet and knocked it right over his nose! He swung round at once, in a great rage. When he saw Tippy and Heyho dancing round in joy, he stared in astonishment. What! They had actually dared to throw potatoes at him, the village policeman!

He shook his fist at them angrily. "You just wait, you little wretches!" he cried. "I'll come round for you this evening! If I wasn't warning everyone to keep indoors for a few hours, till a bear, an elephant, a kangaroo and a lion are caught, I'd come after you now! I only hope you'll meet all the animals that have escaped from the travelling circus – you'll get a fine fright then!"

Tippy and Heyho heard all this – and when Mr Plod had finished they looked very frightened indeed. Mr Plod disappeared round the corner on his way to warn more people of the escaped circus animals, and Heyho and Tippy looked at one another in the greatest alarm.

"Tippy," said Heyho in a very small voice, "it's not a dream after all. Those animals were real – they were the escaped ones."

"Yes," said Tippy, tears beginning to roll down his cheeks. "And we've eaten that cake."

"And thrown plums at Mrs Surly," said Heyho, still more alarmed.

"And knocked Mr Plod's helmet crooked," said Tippy, sniffing hard. "Fancy – it's not a dream after all. Whatever are we going to do?"

"We shall have to explain to Aunt Minnie that we really and truly thought we *were* in a dream," said Heyho.

"Well, it's the truth," said Tippy, cheering up a little. "She ought to believe us if we are telling the truth."

But, alas, Aunt Minnie didn't believe a word of it!

"Pretending to me that you thought you were in a dream, and so you ate my cake!" she snorted. "You go along and empty your money-boxes and go straight back and buy another cake.

And what's all this about throwing plums at Mrs Surly? She's been round here complaining about you again. I suppose you thought you were still in a dream when you threw the plums!"

"Yes," said Heyho and Tippy. "You *might* believe us, Aunt Minnie, when we tell the truth."

"If you want people to believe you, you shouldn't tell naughty stories as you so often do," said Aunt Minnie. "Who said they hadn't broken that jug

141

yesterday? That was a story, wasn't it? How am I to know this isn't a story, too? Now, you go straight round to Mrs Surly and apologise, and then go and buy another cake with your own money."

"But she'll hit us with her stick," said Tippy.

"You pretend it's just a dream then," said Aunt Minnie. "You're good at that, it seems to me!"

But, alas, it wasn't any good pretending it was a dream when Mrs Surly whacked them with her stick. And the worst of it is they haven't yet seen Mr Plod. But he won't forget to go round to Aunt Minnie's about those potatoes, and goodness knows what will happen to Tippy and Heyho then!

They are being so very, very good now that Aunt Minnie simply can't understand it! I wonder how long it will last!

"Oh, Bother Granny!"

Philip and Margaret lived quite near to their granny's house. Granny was a little old lady who walked with a stick because she had a bad leg. She was Daddy's mother, and often came to see them all.

Philip and Margaret were asked to tea at Granny's once a week. The old lady baked special biscuits for them, and made special peppermint sweets, but they weren't always very nice about going to Granny's.

"Oh, bother!" Philip would say. "Mother, need I go today? I do want to go and sail my ship with Harry."

"You can do that tomorrow," Mother would answer. "You know how Granny likes to see you. And, Margaret dear, be sure to offer to run any errands for Granny. You know she can't get about much with her bad leg."

"Oh, bother Granny!" said Margaret, when Mother had gone. "We're always having to do things for her. It's a pity we're the only grandchildren that live near her. George and Jane are lucky to live too far away to have to waste time on her."

"Yes, they are," said Philip, gloomily. "And, you know, it's Granny's birthday soon – we'll have to take some of our money from our moneybox and buy her a present. And I was saving up for a watch!"

"Granny's a nuisance," said Margaret.

But Granny wasn't really a nuisance. She was a dear little old lady, kind and gentle, and she loved Philip and Margaret very much. She was sad when they seemed sulky and cross the next time they came to see her.

"No thank you," said Philip, when she offered him some biscuits. "I'm

tired of those."

And Margaret said she didn't like peppermints any more. They ran off at the very earliest moment, just as Granny was getting out the snap cards. What a shame!

Now the next day Granny had a letter that pleased her very much. It was from her other son, and he said that he had bought a house not far from Granny, and he and his wife, and George and Jane, his children, were coming to live there the very next week!

145

Granny was so overjoyed that she put on her hat, found her stick, and went tap-tapping along to the house where Philip and Margaret lived to tell the good news.

The family were sitting out in the garden, and Mother was shelling peas. Margaret and Philip hadn't offered to help. They never did!

Just as Granny was going to step out into the garden to call to them, Mother gave a little cry of annoyance.

"Oh dear! I quite forgot to take Granny her coat – the one I got from the cleaners for her yesterday – and I know she wants to wear it tomorrow. Margaret dear, will you go and get it and slip up the road with it?"

"Oh, *Mother*! You know I want to finish this book!" said Margaret. "You're always telling me to do this and that for Granny. She's a nuisance."

"Margaret! How rude and unkind!" said her mother, shocked. "Philip, will *you* take the coat then? Granny's so sweet and kind to you both, surely you

146

can do little things for her now and again."

"Oh, *bother* Granny!" said Philip, and shut his book with a slam. "You make us go and have tea with her every week, and we have to keep on doing this and..."

"Philip, one more word from you and I shall tell your father," said his mother, grieved and upset, "I had no idea you were not fond of Granny. I'm ashamed of you both."

Poor Granny! She heard every single word. She couldn't believe her ears. She

147

stood on the step behind them only a metre or two away, and nobody knew she was there.

The old lady turned and went quietly away. A tear trickled down her cheek. So the children thought she was a bother! They didn't love her. She was just a nuisance. How was it she hadn't guessed that before?

She went home, leaving her news untold. She cheered up a little when she thought of George and Jane coming to live near her. Perhaps they wouldn't think she was such a nuisance. Dear,

dear, she must never ask Margaret and Philip to do anything for her again. She couldn't even ask them to come to tea, now that she knew it was a bore to them. She remembered how they had refused her biscuits and homemade sweets last time. "Oh dear – to think I'm such a nuisance and didn't know it!" said poor Granny.

Well, after that Granny didn't ask Margaret and Philip for anything.

She didn't even ask them to tea each week. Mother thought it was because she was helping her other son and his wife to settle into their new home.

"I expect she's offered to have George and Jane for a bit till their parents are settled in," said Mother. "She was out when I went yesterday – gone to see how the new house was getting on. Quite an excitement for Granny."

"Jolly good thing Granny's got somebody else to fuss round," said Philip to Margaret when they were alone. "Now we needn't bother!"

So they neither of them went near

Granny at all. Then one day George and Jane came to tea. At teatime they told Philip's mother that Granny was taking them to the Zoo the next day.

"We were hoping that Philip and Margaret were coming too," said Jane.

"They haven't been asked," said Mother, looking a bit puzzled. "In fact, I don't think Granny has asked them to her house, even, for quite a long time."

"We go there to tea twice a week," said Jane. "We do love it. We didn't know Granny very well before, and she's the only Granny we've got. Isn't she a darling old lady?"

"Yes, she's very kind," said Mother.

"She always makes us something exciting," said George. "Yesterday we had little gingerbread men, and on Friday she's making us jelly. And did you know she's given us that little man who nods his head? Jane loved it so much that she made her have it."

"And she gave George a lovely spade," said Jane. "But he deserved it, Aunt, because he went and weeded her front garden beautifully. He did it for a surprise. I suppose Philip and Margaret are going to Granny's party on Saturday? It's her birthday and she's having a cake with seventy-two candles on – fancy that!"

Philip and Margaret felt more and more uncomfortable, and Mother felt more and more surprised. Why, Granny was seeing far more of George and Jane than she had ever seen of Philip and Margaret – and how very, very nicely

the children talked of their granny. No
wonder she asked them so often, and
gave them treats. The days went on,
and Granny didn't ask Philip and
Margaret to her birthday party, or even
to tea, or to see her. They took her little
presents, but she was out. She wrote
them a little note of thanks each, but
that was all.

It was a lovely birthday party, George
told Philip. "There was a conjurer!" he
said. "Fancy an old lady thinking of a
conjurer for a party! She told us to
bring two school friends and we did.
Why didn't you come? Don't you like
Granny? We think she's a darling."

Philip went red. He was feeling very much ashamed of himself now, and so was Margaret. They could see very well how much nicer George and Jane were to Granny than they had ever been. They had taken her kindness for granted, had hardly ever thanked her for anything, and had been very rude.

"Well – we used to think Granny was a bit of a nuisance," said Philip, at last, seeing that George was expecting him to answer.

"Gracious! How horrid of you! She's such an old lady and she's your *Granny*!" said Jane in shocked tones.

"Oh, well – it's a good thing *we* like her - we can do some of the things you don't want to do. Does she know you think she's a nuisance? I think she must know, because she never, never asks you to do anything for her now, does she?'

"No," said Margaret. "I don't expect she loves us any more, now you've come. You're so much nicer to her." When Jane and George had gone, Philip looked at Margaret. "This is awful," he said. "I feel terribly mean.

But we can't possibly start fussing round Granny again now because she'll only think it's because we're jealous of George and Jane."

"All the same, I'm going to do *something*!" said Margaret. "I can't bear feeling mean like this. I know! Let's get up early every single morning before Granny is up and go round to her kitchen garden and weed it! She won't know who's done it and we won't tell her – but it will be a way of making up for being horrid."

So, every morning at seven o'clock, the two children went secretly round to Granny's. They weeded her kitchen garden really well. They didn't know that Granny, who always woke early, watched them each morning from her bedroom window.

One morning, just as they were slipping away at eight o'clock, Granny called them. They went to her, red in the face.

"Well, my dears, I've been watching you – and you're very kind – but why do you bother with an old lady who is just a nuisance? You see, I couldn't help hearing what you both said about me one day in your garden – and I do see that I'm a nuisance to you."

"Oh, Granny, you're *not*! It was only us that were so horrid!" said Margaret. "You're not a nuisance to George and Jane – they love you. And you're not a nuisance to us, either. It was just that we were horrid and selfish."

"So we've been trying to make up for it – but we didn't mean you to know it was us," said Philip. "We came each morning. Can we go on coming?"

"Yes – if you will come to tea next time George and Jane come," said Granny, looking suddenly very happy. "And if you will come to the Zoo with me – and let me give you some of my new chocolate buns to taste."

"We'd *love* to!" said Margaret, giving Granny a hug. "And please, please, Granny, let *us* run your errands sometimes and not always George and Jane. We do want to as well."

So now Granny has four grandchildren she loves, and who love her. She thinks she's very lucky – but all four think they're luckier still to have such a kind, gentle old lady for a granny!

157

The Other
Little Boy

Ronnie was a very naughty little boy.
He was rude and unkind to his mother,
and he would have been rude to his
father if he had dared to be. He was
rude to the daily help, and he always
put out his tongue at the little girl next
door.

"Ronnie! Why do you behave so
badly?" his mother would say. "You
make me very sad. I can't believe that
you are my little boy when you do
things like that."

Ronnie banged the door when he was
in a temper. He kicked the legs of his
chair when he was cross at table. He
turned up his nose at all the things he
didn't like, and shouted for the things
he did like.

"One day, Ronnie, I shall get another little boy," said his mother. "I don't think you are a very nice little boy to have. If you go on behaving like this, I think I shall have to look out for another little boy."

"All right," said Ronnie. "I don't care."

He felt quite certain that his mother didn't mean it. It was just one of the things that grown-ups said but didn't mean at all.

So you can just imagine his enormous astonishment when he came home from school one day to find another little boy with his mother! This little boy was a

159

bit bigger than Ronnie, and he was fair instead of being dark. His smiling face was freckled all over.

"Who are you?" said Ronnie.

"I'm Dan," said the other boy.

"You go away," said Ronnie fiercely, "or I'll fight you!"

"I'm bigger than you, and I've learnt boxing, so I should win," said Dan.

"Dan!" called Ronnie's mother. "Will you come and help me for a minute?"

"Coming!" called Dan, and rushed off at once. Ronnie's mother was sorting out newspapers for salvage. She was smoothing out the papers till they were flat and then packing them into a box. "I'll help you. I'd love to," said Dan.

"Thank you, Dan," said Ronnie's mother, and smiled at him.

Ronnie rushed up at once. "I'll do it," he said.

"No, Ronnie," said his mother. "I've so often asked you to do this little job for me, and you've grumbled and never done it. Now Dan and I will do it together."

"I'll do it," said Ronnie again.

"You do what your mother tells you!" said Dan. "She and I can do this nicely together. You go and play."

"Who's this horrid boy?" Ronnie demanded, turning to his mother. "Send him away."

"Certainly not," said his mother. "Dan has no mother at all. He has never had all the things you have had –

161

the joy of helping his mother, having her kiss him goodnight, telling her his troubles, looking after her when she is tired, sharing everything with her. You don't want those things, Ronnie, and you said you wouldn't mind if I got another little boy."

"What about *me*?" said Ronnie, feeling terribly angry and hurt.

"Well, you can do what you like," said his mother. "You can go to Dan's home for a bit, if you like – or you can go to boarding-school – or you can stay here if you don't interfere with Dan. He is going to look after me now and help me."

Ronnie could hardly believe his ears. He stared at his mother and frowned at Dan. Then he fled from the room and slammed the door so that the house shook.

He went to find his father. "I don't want this Dan in my house," he stormed. "I won't have Mother looking after him!"

"My dear Ronnie, surely you can see

that Dan is the kind of boy who will look after your mother, and not expect her to look after *him* all the time!" said his father. "It's your own fault. I don't blame your mother for choosing another little boy. She's a darling and so kind and jolly. She's wasted on *you* – but a boy like Dan knows what a treasure she is, and will love her with all his heart. I must say I rather like Dan myself."

Ronnie felt as if he was in a dream. How awful to come home and suddenly find another boy there, taking his place, and everyone liking him!

"Don't you like *me*, Daddy?" he asked, his voice beginning to tremble. "Don't you love me?"

"I love you, because you are my son," said his father, "but I can't say I *like* you very much, Ronnie. Why should I? You are rude and selfish and unkind. I shall always love you and back you up, but whether I like you or not depends on yourself and your own behaviour."

Ronnie ran upstairs to his room. He was so angry and upset and shocked that he sat in a chair and sobbed. He sobbed loudly, but his mother didn't come to him. He heard voices in the garden, and saw his mother and Dan there, his mother showing Dan where the logs were kept.

"If you would bring me in twelve every day, Dan, that would be a great help," she said.

"I'd love to," said Dan, and slipped his hand inside Ronnie's mother's arm. Ronnie sobbed again. How often had his mother asked him if he would bring logs up each day for her fire, and he hadn't bothered to remember? Now this horrible boy was going to remember and never once forget!

Ronnie saw Dan carrying logs. He was alone. Ronnie rushed down to him in the garden and shouted at him.

"You leave those logs alone! That's my job."

"Now, now," said Dan. "I promised your mother I'd take some in. I say, isn't she a lovely mother to have? I wish I had one like that. She's so kind and loving. I'd do anything in the world for her!"

"You go away or I'll fight you," said

Ronnie fiercely. Dan laughed. Ronnie
hit him hard on the shoulder. Then he
suddenly saw a very different Dan –
and felt one too! Dan hit out with his
fists, first the right and then the left –
and Ronnie found himself on his back,

his chin smarting and his left ear tingling.

"I warned you not to fight me," said Dan, picking up a log and walking to the house. Ronnie picked himself up and ran howling to his mother. But she sided with Dan.

"Don't be a baby," she said. "And don't howl like that. I have a headache." Ronnie howled all the more. Dan looked fierce again. "Did you hear what your mother said?" he asked. "I won't have her worried when she's got a headache. If you want to make a noise, go outside!"

And to Ronnie's enormous rage, Dan took hold of his arm and pushed him out into the hall! "Thank you, Dan dear," he heard his mother say. "I really can't bear that noise."

Ronnie went to his room and stayed there till supper. He didn't go down to tea. He thought his mother would come up to him, but she didn't. So he went without tea. He heard everyone laughing and talking downstairs in the

dining-room. He pictured to himself Dan offering his mother the jam and the cake, looking after her all the time. They didn't want Ronnie. He was just a horrid, selfish, rude boy. Nobody wanted him!

He went down to supper. "Hallo, Ronnie!" said his father, and the others smiled at him. They didn't say anything at all about him missing his tea. Dan talked to Ronnie's father and mother happily, and made all kinds of jokes. He really was a very jolly, kindly boy, and Ronnie would have liked him very much at any other time. He was very sweet to Ronnie's mother and looked after her all the time.

"I must say it's nice to see a boy with good manners," said Ronnie's father, beaming at Dan.

At bedtime Dan went to bed in the spare room. Ronnie undressed gloomily. He couldn't think what he was to do. This boy seemed to have come to live there. He certainly was a nice boy, just the kind his mother loved – just the kind *any* mother would love!

"And I'm just the kind any mother would dislike, I suppose!" thought Ronnie. He got into bed and waited for his mother to come and say goodnight to him. But she didn't come. She went to tuck up Dan. Ronnie heard her say: "Oh, Dan, what a hug! You've almost taken my breath away!"

For the next few days Dan made things very pleasant indeed for Ronnie's mother and father. He was

such a jolly boy, and always so willing to do anything for anyone. Even the daily help sang his praises, and as for the little girl next door, she thought Dan was wonderful because he had made her a doll out of a fir-cone and an oak-apple and twigs!

Ronnie didn't try to fight Dan again. He knew that was no use. He didn't

170

try sulking or howling, because if he sulked no one took any notice of him, and if he howled Dan pushed him out of the room. So, for once, he was a quiet, polite boy, and sometimes even played with Dan.

Dan talked a lot about Ronnie's mother. "Isn't she marvellous!" he said to Ronnie. "Of course, you've had her all your life, but I've never had a mother. Mine died when I was a day old. I tell you, it's wonderful to have someone like a mother, looking so sweet and being so kind and loving always."

Ronnie looked at his mother. She did look sweet, sitting there sewing, her dark, curly head bent, and her brown eyes following her needle. Ronnie suddenly felt as if he badly wanted to do something for her.

"But I suppose she would much rather let Dan do something for her," he thought. All the same, he went over to his mother and put his hand in hers. She looked up, surprised.

"Would you like me to do anything

for you, Mother?" asked Ronnie. "Do you want anything fetched? Would you like another cushion?"

"Yes, I would," said his mother. Ronnie fetched another cushion.

"Thank you, dear," she said and smiled at him. Ronnie wanted to hug her, but he was afraid she wouldn't like him to, now she had Dan.

The next day Ronnie fetched and carried everything he could for his mother, and Dan looked at him in astonishment.

"I say!" said Dan that evening. "I believe you could look after that nice mother of yours properly if you really wanted to."

"Of course I could!" said Ronnie indignantly. He looked at Dan and went red. "I don't like the way you've taken my mother away from me," he said. "I know I was beastly to her before – I see that, now I've watched how you behave to her, and I can see how much she likes you, and I don't wonder. Are you going to live here always?"

"Well, I'd rather like to get back home soon," said Dan. "I've got a sister at home who wants a bit of looking after – but I don't want to leave your mother unless you are going to make her happy. I really do love her, and even if I go home I shall often come and see her. I wish she were mine. I can't think why you don't love her. I think she's a darling."

"I *do* love her," said Ronnie fiercely. "You go back home, Dan, and come again in a week's time. You just see if I

173

can't look after my own mother and love her just as you do – more, because I'm her own boy and you're not!"

"All right," said Dan. "I'll go. But listen, Ronnie. If you make her unhappy, I'll come back again!"

Dan went the next day, and he often comes back to see Ronnie and Ronnie's mother. She always looks happy now, and tells Dan what a fine boy Ronnie is – and, strange to say, Ronnie and Dan are great friends!

"You'll never get another little boy now, will you, Mother?" Ronnie says at night, when his mother kisses him goodnight. And she always says the same thing. "Never, Ronnie! You're the only one I want!"

And that's very nice for them both, isn't it?

What Happened
on Christmas Eve

"Now – are we all ready?" asked Santa Claus, standing by his reindeer sleigh. "Sack in? All the toys in it that I asked for – especially those new aeroplanes for the boys? Have the reindeer had a good feed?"

"Yes, sir," said his little servant. "Look at them stamping their feet and tossing their antlers in the air! They are longing to go. Goodbye, sir; I hope you have a good journey. You will find you have plenty of toys in the sack, and you know the spell to use if you want some more."

"Right," said Santa Claus and stepped into his sleigh. "Brrrrrr! It's a cold and frosty night. Pull the rug closely round my feet, please."

He was well tucked-in. He took the reins and clicked to the four impatient reindeer. "Get along, then! Up into the air with you – and for goodness' sake look out for telegraph wires before you land on anyone's roof!"

Bells began to ring very loudly as the reindeer galloped over the snow and then rose smoothly in the air, their feet still galloping. Only reindeer belonging to Santa Claus could gallop through the air. They loved that. It was a wonderful feeling.

They soon left the sky over Toyland and galloped into the sky over our land. The moon sailed up and lighted everything. Santa Claus peered downwards.

"We're there! Go a bit lower, reindeer, I must just look at my notebook to see the names there."

"Peter Jones, Sara White, Ben White, Michael Andrews ... they all live somewhere here. Land on a roof nearby, reindeer."

The reindeer galloped downwards. The biggest one looked out for telegraph wires. The year before he had caught his hoofs in some and had nearly upset the sleigh. He guided the others safely down to a big roof, where a large chimney stood.

Santa Claus got out and pulled his sack from the sleigh. "Two children here," he said. "Sara and Ben White. Good children, too. I shall leave them some nice toys."

177

He disappeared down the chimney. The reindeer waited patiently. One of them began to paw at the roof, and then stopped quickly. He remembered that he had been told never to do that. It might wake up the children of the house if they heard someone knocking on the roof!

The breath of the reindeer looked like steam in the frosty, moonlit air. They stood and stared out over the quiet town. This was a big adventure for them, and they enjoyed every minute of it.

Santa Claus popped his head out of the chimney. "Give me a pull," he said to the biggest reindeer.

The reindeer turned his big head and put his mouth down to Santa Claus's neck. He tugged at the back of his cloak there, and Santa Claus came up with a jerk, his sack after him.

"Thanks," he said. "I must have got a bit fatter. I never stuck in that chimney before. The two children were fast asleep, reindeer. They *have* grown since last year. The girl has stopped biting her nails. I noticed that. I gave her a specially nice doll because I felt so pleased."

"Hrrrrumph," said the reindeer, sounding pleased too. In a minute or two they were all galloping off at top speed again, the bells jingling.

Santa Claus was very busy. He left toys here, there and everywhere. Then he came to a little village and peered downwards. "There are two children somewhere down there," he said. "Let me see – what were their names? Ah, yes – Elizabeth and Jonathan. Now – where's my notebook? What shall I leave them this year?"

He turned the pages and looked down a list of names. "Oh dear! The report I had of them this year isn't good. They've been rude to their mother – and have been lazy at school. I'm afraid I can't leave them anything. And they did seem such nice children last year. What a pity! Reindeer – go on to the next big town, please. There are a lot of children there."

And then something happened. An aeroplane came flying by, fairly low, just as the reindeer galloped upwards into the frosty sky. There wasn't a collision because the biggest reindeer swerved at once – but the aeroplane caused such a tremendous current of air, as it passed close to the sleigh, that Santa Claus felt

himself being blown off! He clutched at the side of the sleigh and just managed to hold on, though his legs were blown over the side and he had to climb back very carefully indeed.

He sat down and mopped his forehead. "My word! What a narrow escape!" he said. "I feel quite faint. Go slowly to the next town, reindeer. I've had a fright."

So they went very slowly indeed, and Santa Claus lay back in his rugs and got over the shock. He didn't know that his sack of toys had been blown right out of the sleigh!

It had risen in the air when the aeroplane almost bumped into them, and had then dropped downwards. It

landed with a tremendous thud on the roof of a house, burst open, and flung all the toys inside to the ground. They rolled down the roof one by one – ships, dolls, balls, teddy bears, trains and all.

Bumpity-bump! Clitter-clat! Rilloby-roll! Down they went and fell all over the garden below.

The two children in the house were wide awake. They hadn't been to sleep at all. They were Elizabeth and Jonathan Frost, the two children that Santa Claus was not going to give any toys to because their school reports had

182

been bad, and because they had been so rude to their mother that year.

They hadn't been able to go to sleep because they were unhappy. Their mother was ill in hospital – just at Christmastime! Nothing could be worse.

"I wouldn't feel so bad about it if only we hadn't been so horrid to Mother," said Jonathan. "She never said a word about being ill – and we kept on being rude. Whatever came over us to be so horrid?"

"I don't know," said Elizabeth. "And now we've upset Daddy too, because our bad school reports came on the very day Mother went to hospital – just as if he hadn't already had too much bad luck. I feel awful. I wish we'd had good reports to cheer up poor Daddy."

"There won't be any presents this Christmas," said Jonathan gloomily. "Mother away – Daddy upset. Nobody will think about us at all."

"Well, Mrs Brown next door said it served us right to have a miserable

Christmas," said Elizabeth. "She said she'd heard us being cheeky to Mother. And she said if we hadn't been so horrid to poor Mother, she would have bought us presents herself, but she didn't think we deserved any."

"Well, we don't," said Jonathan. "We've been simply ... I say! What's that noise? It sounds like bells!"

It *was* bells. The children listened. Then they heard another sound. "An aeroplane!" said Elizabeth. "Isn't it low? I wonder what those bells were."

Suddenly there was a tremendous thud on the roof. Crash! Then came lots of other, smaller noises. *Bumpity-bump! Clitter-clat! Rilloby-roll!*

The children sat up straight and looked out of the window. In the moonlight they saw a lot of little dark things falling. Whatever was happening?

"What is it?" said Jonathan, scared. "Something fell on the roof. Do you think it was something the aeroplane dropped? Shall we go and look?"

"Yes," said Elizabeth, scrambling out of bed. She dragged on her thick robe and put on warm slippers. "Quick! Come and see."

They went down the stairs and opened the back door. Scattered all over the garden were many little dark things. Elizabeth picked up the first one and looked at it in the moonlight.

"Jonathan! It's a doll! The prettiest one I ever saw in my life. Do look!"

But Jonathan was picking up a train – and a big ship with magnificent sails – and three teddy-bears in a row

185

together! Elizabeth began to pick up things, too. Another doll – two fat toy pandas – a doll's house with its chimney off – a musical box. Really there seemed to be no end to the toys in their garden that night!

The children piled them all together and went through them again. What a wonderful collection! Elizabeth nursed each of the dolls, and Jonathan wound up the train to see if the clockwork was still all right.

"*Where* did they come from? Did that aeroplane really drop them?" said Elizabeth.

"No, I don't think so," said Jonathan. "You know, Elizabeth, I think Santa

Claus must have galloped over here and he's dropped his sack of toys. Look up on the roof. That looks like a big, burst-open sack there, doesn't it?"

It did. The children stared at it. "Well – I suppose we can't keep any of these lovely things then," said Elizabeth with a sigh. "I do love this baby doll so much. What shall we do with everything?"

"I expect when Santa Claus misses his sack, he will come back and look for it," said Jonathan. "We had better put everything into one of our own sacks –

187

there are plenty in the shed. We will leave it standing in the garden for him to see. He will easily spot it in the moonlight."

"I wish we could keep just one thing each," said Elizabeth.

"Well, we can't," said Jonathan. "For one thing the toys aren't ours. And for another thing you know jolly well we don't deserve anything."

They found a big sack and put everything into it. Just as they were

tying up the neck, they heard the sound of bells again – and there, up in the bright moonlit sky, they saw the reindeer sleigh, and Santa Claus leaning over, looking downwards. He saw the children, of course, and down he came, the reindeer landing softly in the garden snow.

"Your sack fell on our roof!" said Jonathan, running up to help him out of the sleigh. "We've collected all the toys, sir, and put them into another sack. Here they are!"

"What good, honest children!" beamed Santa Claus, taking the big sack from them. "I'm sure I must have your names down on my list. I'll let you *choose* your Christmas toys, for being such a help. Let me see, what *are* your names?"

"Elizabeth and Jonathan, Santa Claus," said Elizabeth. Santa Claus at once looked solemn.

"Oh! I'm sorry – your names are *not* down on my list for presents this year. Bad work at school – and rudeness to your mother. What a pity!"

The children went red. "Yes," said Jonathan. "It's more than a pity, Santa Claus. Our mother's ill and in hospital, and we can't forgive ourselves for making her unhappy. And our father has just had our bad reports when he's feeling miserable about Mother. I can tell you we're going to turn over a new leaf next year!"

"Yes, we're both going to be top of our forms, and we're going to make such a fuss of Mother when she comes home that she will be happier than she's ever been before!" said Elizabeth. "We didn't expect any presents from you this year. We haven't even hung our stockings up."

"Well – it's good to see children who are not ashamed to own up when they've done wrong," said Santa Claus. "I think I'd better leave you two little things, just as a reward for picking up all my toys for me."

"We'd rather you left Mother something at the hospital," said

Jonathan. "She broke her watch the day before she was ill. Could you leave her a new one, do you think?"

"Oh yes!" said Santa Claus. "I'll do that. Goodbye and thank you – and just see that I have your names down on my list for *next* Christmas!"

He drove off into the air with a jingling of bells, and the children went to bed, feeling sleepy. They were fast asleep in two minutes.

In the morning, what a surprise! Standing at the end of Elizabeth's bed was the big baby doll she had picked up the night before – and at the end of Jonathan's was the toy train!

"He came back! Oh, he's the kindest old fellow in the world!" cried Elizabeth. "Jonathan, I do hope he remembered Mother's watch."

He did, of course. She was even more surprised than the children to find such a lovely present by her bedside – and one that nobody knew anything about at all!

"Well, that was an adventure that did a lot of good!" said Santa Claus, as he galloped back to Toyland that night. "It's nice to meet children who know how to turn over a new leaf. What a surprise they'll get on Christmas morning! I wonder if their names will be down on my list for next Christmas."

Of course they will, Santa Claus! We can all tell you that for certain!